SAGEBRUSH KNIGHT

A FANCIFUL JOURNEY

EVERETT RIGGS

RUBY VALLEY PRESS

To my Family, Uncle Jack, and my supporters

BUNKHOUSE

The blistering sun beat down on the J-Bar-T Ranch with a punishing glare, causing everything in sight to shimmer with the heat. A wind kicked up dust, swirling it about like smoke from a campfire. Even the birds were silent under the blazing sky. The ranch looked abandoned. Not a living soul was moving about, everyone waiting for the sun to take its rest.

The year was 1910, and the days of the Old West were fading into memory. The old order had worked well for the denizens of this central part of Montana, but times were changing—not all were happy about it. It had been many years since outlaws and others not accustomed to living by established order had openly operated in the area. Civilization was establishing its firm grip. And along with that came all the apparatus of government, imprinting itself like a boot stomping on a grasshopper.

The J-Bar-T was in a low spot along the American Fork of the Musselshell River. Trees and growth around the small stream afforded some protection from the relentless wind and elements that blasted the surrounding plains in all seasons, but the foliage could not offer complete respite. The Crazy, Little Belts and Big Snowy Mountains stood guard over the area, silent observers to all that occurred there.

The pulsing artery of life in the area was the Musselshell River. From its beginning at the confluence of the North Fork and South Fork near Martinsdale, the river meandered and wound its way through the broad, open valley of windswept prairie. Its banks choked with brush in many places in the upper reaches and lined with willow and cottonwood trees throughout the valley. Grass was abundant, nourishing both livestock and wildlife. The people had built towns near the river, and the railroad also followed its trail.

Primarily a sheep operation, the J-Bar-T housed some cattle for commercial and personal use. The sheep were Merino, a Spanish breed with fat legs and wooly coats that produced a much-valued fine wool. Their brilliant fleece would often turn iridescent in the sunlight, flashing threads of gold and silver as they lazily grazed across the great expanse of prairie. Little ships of treasure bobbing across an ocean of green and brown.

INSIDE THE BUNKHOUSE on the ranch, three men wiled away their time. Each man sat in a shaded area of the roughly built structure, away from the windows, believing the shade the building offered would provide some relief from the heat. It offered none, but the men were in fine spirits. Any time off work was good, even if it sometimes led to trouble. The ranch hands could find salvation or dissipation in equal measure in the churches and saloons of the area, depending on an individual's mood. It didn't require a genius to determine the likely path chosen by hired hands with free time to burn. On this day, however, it was just too hot to even think about venturing into town.

On a small bed in the bunkhouse's corner, Little Jimmy sat strumming an old, battered guitar. He was young and tiny, not even reaching the average height of adulthood. Never still, his skinny body constantly shifted and fidgeted. Jimmy's clothes were always dirt-stained and ragged. His matted hair, tangled from days of not washing, hung limply around his thin cheeks and neck, tarnishing his otherwise dull complexion. The other hired hands often took it upon themselves to dunk him in the creek now and then to get rid of some of the stench. Despite his deplorable state, Jimmy was well-liked by the others on the ranch.

Seated at a table was an older Mexican man known as the Professor because of his ability to read well and tell engaging stories that seemed to impart great wisdom. He also spoke English with confidence, which impressed everyone on the ranch. Unlike Little Jimmy, the Professor took pride in his appearance, and was always clean and neatly dressed.

Across from the Professor, a tall cowboy, sandy-haired with a lanky build, flipped a pocketknife into the wall of the bunkhouse while balancing on a rickety chair. His chiseled, handsome face, that had a small white scar on the point of the chin, was tanned but too young to have been deeply weathered by the elements yet. The scar gave him character, or at least he thought so, but his most striking feature was his green eyes. His slouched posture and the lazy way in which he tossed the knife into the wall exuded boredom.

Colt Matson was twenty-five years old. He had been working on ranches since he was fifteen and had found his way to the J-Bar-T three years prior. He fancied himself a genuine cowboy of the Old West, a holdout among a dying breed. Whereas the other men on the ranch wore practical clothing for their tasks and could roughly pass as cowboys, Colt dressed in the full regalia of the open-range cowboy.

He always wore step-in shotgun chaps with pockets on the front. A large wide-brimmed hat with a three-dent crown adorned his head, and he usually tied a bright silk bandana around his neck. The Mexican rowels on the spurs attached to his stovepipe boots jingled loudly whenever he walked. But his pride and joy was the pearl-handled peacemaker he carried on his hip. He only took it off to sleep, resting the gun on the bed next to him as he slept.

The other men found his look somewhat comical. They refrained from teasing him openly because of Colt's unnerving habit of pulling his pistol on the men whenever he took offense to something. They didn't believe he would fire the weapon, but one didn't know for sure, and an accident was always a possibility. Still, the men tolerated him and indulged his eccentricities. They noted he possessed fine skills as a cowboy, although those skills were not in high demand on a sheep ranch, and that he was a hard worker.

Colt took a break from throwing the knife into the wall and looked over at Little Jimmy. His cheeks tightened, like he had tasted something sour. "Jimmy, you can't play that guitar worth a damn."

Jimmy stopped strumming the guitar and

sat up straight, offended at Colt's assessment of his playing ability. He stared at Colt for a moment. "I'm pretty new to the guitar business, Colt. Give a feller a chance!"

Colt rubbed his chin and looked at the floor, thinking. Then he looked up, slapped himself on the knee and said, "Well, Jimmy, I got a little song in my head. Let me start it, and you try to follow along."

Jimmy smiled and readied his guitar. "Alright, Colt."

Colt cleared his throat and set a steady boot tap on the floor. His spurs jingled in time to the rhythm as he picked up the pace, tapping out the beat on his knee. Jimmy's expression brightened further, and he moved over to the edge of his bed, bringing his feet down onto the floor and joining Colt in syncopated tapping along with the Professor, whose head was moving in time with the beat. The tempo increased and Colt began humming. Jimmy quickly joined him on the guitar. As the beat continued, all three men swayed and moved to the rhythm of the music.

Then Colt abruptly stopped and looked at

his companions. He shrugged and said, "That's all I got right now."

Jimmy looked confused. "That's all you got? What kind of song is that? You ain't got any words. A song has to have words, Colt. That song of yours needs a little work."

Colt fired back, "What the hell do you know about songs, Jimmy? It's not like you're making money pickin' that guitar."

"I didn't know a man could make money pickin' guitars. I thought you just did it for fun."

Colt softened and smiled. "Sure, you can make money at it. I met a fella over in the saloon in Shawmut who claimed he made money playing songs on his guitar. He said he'd set himself up with a bottle of whiskey and just start playing. Said he had a man with him who'd lost a leg in a farm accident and couldn't work no more. The man would do a jig every few songs. People would throw a little money in a hat to see it."

Jimmy sat back as though someone had pushed him, and his eyebrows raised as he considered what Colt had said. "I'll be! I would've paid a little to see that. How would a one-legged man do a jig?"

Colt threw his hands up. "How do I know? I imagine he just hopped around a little. Drunks in a saloon will pay to see damn near anything."

Jimmy was hooked, and he squirmed as he said, "I might have to get into that kind of business. It beats working on a sheep outfit. Did he make a lot of money at it?"

Colt tilted his head and thought for a moment. "Judging by the amount of whiskey he drank, he did pretty well at it, although he didn't do any guitar playing when I saw him."

Jimmy suddenly looked sad and softly asked Colt, "What happened to the one-legged man?"

"I can't say. The fella didn't say why he wasn't with him anymore. This is pretty tough country for a one-legged man. I suspect things didn't end well for him."

Jimmy lowered his head and went silent, contemplating the fate of the one-legged man. Colt flicked his knife back into the wall and said, "I'm bored, boys. Bored with life."

Little Jimmy perked up. "Why don't you go down to the creek and do some fishing?"

"There ain't nothing but sucker fish in that creek."

Jimmy stiffened. He vigorously disagreed with Colt. "That's not true! I've caught some nice trout in there!"

Colt dismissively flicked a hand at Jimmy. "Good for you. I never cared much for fishing. I don't like to eat trout."

The gesture didn't deter Jimmy. "They are good eatin' if the water is cold."

Colt rolled his eyes and said, "Good grief, Jimmy, you could take a warm bath in that creek right now."

He then looked over at the Professor, who was intently reading a book.

"Professor, how did a Mexican come to be here? Seems like Mexican folks might be a little put off by the cold weather and all. What are you reading in that fancy book?"

The Professor marked his page and placed the book on the table. He was an average-sized man with gray speckled hair. Years of living and working outdoors were etched into his cheeks and around his eyes, but it gave him the appearance of being wise rather than old. The primary feature of his face was a long, prominent nose. He was fit and lean, as were most who worked on the ranches in the area.

He looked Colt straight in the eye, leaned forward and said, "Mexican people aren't scared of cold, you fool. There are many Mexican people in Montana. We are tough and brave. I came up the trail from Texas with the cattle herds when the land was wild and free. It wasn't that long ago. Not even the life of a man has passed since those days. I was raised to be a vaquero."

The Professor smiled, thinking back to his youth. "I rode with the real cowboys, traveling over unknown and dangerous lands. The work was hard. Very hard. George Parrott, the outlaw, even bought me a drink in a saloon in Miles City. People called it Milestown in those days. I found him to be quite agreeable. I cannot speak to his outlaw activities. His end was unfortunate, but such is the life of an outlaw."

Colt interjected, "I'll tell you one thing. This land will be free again if I have any say in the matter."

"Amigo, I suspect you will have little say in the matter, but as for the book, it's about a great hero and adventurer of the Spanish people, Don Quixote."

"It looks like it's written in that Mexican

language. At least the cover of it looks that way."

The Professor now spoke to Colt as though he were addressing an ignorant child. "Yes, it's written in Spanish, one of the great languages of romance."

Colt grinned and looked over at Jimmy. "I've never needed Spanish to do any romancing around here."

The Professor's eyes reflected his disgust. "That is because you've never really had any need for romance. It's unnecessary when all you do is pay for the company of a woman."

Undeterred by Colt's interruptions, the Professor continued. "Don Quixote was a knight who went on many adventures. He fought great battles against impossible odds and rescued many women in distress. Some were even princesses and other ladies of noble blood. Don Quixote was, above all else, a man of chivalry and honor."

Colt spat on the floor. "I don't know nothing about any chivalry business. But the adventurin' sure sounds like fun. Did this Don character ever make any money in the adventurin' business?"

"He most certainly did. He discovered many great treasures during his travels."

Colt's manner changed. He was now keenly interested in what the Professor had to say. "Treasure! Now that sounds like a good deal for a guy like me. How'd this Don character get started in adventurin'? Are there any instructions on it in that book?"

"Don Quixote just did it. There weren't any instructions. He was his own man, and his heart led him on the proper path. A faithful companion accompanied him, mounted on the finest steed."

Colt let out a sigh and said, "Boy, I sure could use a good mount. We ride old plugs and nags around here. It seems like a man would want a good mount to adventure on. But I guess my old horse is alright. He's been with me a spell and is steady. I can do without a companion. I don't want to be forced to cut another man in on the money. There ain't no need to be splitting adventure treasure. Professor, what do you think about me trying to go about adventurin' on my own?"

The Professor shrugged. "It's not for me to say, Colt. That is your choice. The path is in your mind and heart. Each adventurer must choose their own journey in this world."

Colt beamed. "This is gonna be a cinch. I got plenty of ideas spinning around in my head now. I think this adventurin' is really going to suit me. Yes, sir! I'm all for it."

The Professor looked at Colt with a playful smirk and returned to reading.

* * *

THE NEXT DAY, the owner of the J-Bar-T, Jim Evinrude, gathered Colt for a trip to Harlowton. Colt was delighted to venture into what he viewed as the "big town" and could barely contain his enthusiasm. They left early in the morning, intending to stay the night at the Graves Hotel, a beautiful three-story sandstone structure that served as the primary resting place for travelers passing through the region.

Harlowton was the largest town in the area and served as a hub for the Milwaukee Railroad coming from the east. It was the seat of commerce for the region. The town sat on rawhide-colored prairie that sloped down toward the Musselshell River. As the two men rode into the community, Colt gazed at the quaint shops lining the main street, the busy saloons, and the Graves Hotel, prominent among all the other buildings.

Evinrude was coming to town to run errands, but also expected to receive a telegram from his daughter, Janel, who was returning to the family ranch for a brief visit after spending four years in New York City with her aunt, a wealthy woman with connections throughout the New York area.

When they arrived at their destination, Jim Evinrude tied his horse to the hitching rack outside the Graves Hotel and sent Colt to retrieve the telegram from his daughter. The J-Bar-T owner was the embodiment of a cowboy. Grizzled and tough when he needed to be, but kind to those he cared about and those in need. He walked with a hitch in his step from old injuries, his broad shoulders keeping time with his gait as he moved. And he always moved with a sense of purpose, never unsure of what he wanted. The years had added a little paunch around his middle, but he was a man who could still get the job done. Evinrude looked around before entering the hotel and spied a horseless carriage sputtering slowly down the street. He stared at the contraption with disdain for a few moments, then went inside the building.

Once inside, Evinrude headed directly for the saloon area of the hotel. He walked up to the bar and leaned on it. The bartender, a man named Fran, had his back to him and tidied up behind the bar before turning to his customer. Only a couple of other people were in the saloon area, which suited Jim Evinrude.

Fran walked over to Evinrude and said, "Hello, Mr. Evinrude. What are you drinking today?"

Evinrude slapped a hand on the bar and replied, "Hello, Fran. I'm in need of some whiskey. Leave the bottle, please."

"Yes, sir."

Fran quickly grabbed a bottle of whiskey and a glass. He returned to Evinrude, filled the small glass, and set the bottle on the bar.

"What brings you to town, Mr. Evinrude?"

"Oh, I had a couple of errands to run, and I'm waiting for a telegram from Janel. She's coming back to the ranch for a visit from the big city."

Fran clapped his hands together. "That's

great news! She's been gone a spell, hasn't she?"

Evinrude gave the bartender a slight nod. "Sure has. I wonder what she'll think of us now that she's tasted something different. Apparently, she's also bringing two of the New York City relatives back with her. Mary and her boy, Dalton."

Amused by the news, Fran chuckled. "That oughta be interesting. Have either of them ever been to Montana?"

Then, a thought entered Fran's mind, and he became solemn, thinking of the passing of Jim's wife. Everyone in Harlowton had liked her, and she had more than once told stories of her taciturn sister, Mary.

Before Evinrude could answer his question, Fran bowed his head and said, "The last time you saw Mary must have been at your wife's funeral. God rest her soul."

Evinrude grimaced and took a drink. "It's been some time since I've seen Mary, but not long enough. It was at the funeral. Still, I need to show her hospitality, or Susan is likely to rise from the grave and slap me upside the head. It still rankles me I had to take my wife back east to bury her. But that's what she wanted. She made me promise before she passed, even though I don't think she was in her right mind, being close to death and very feverish to boot."

The grizzled cowboy took another drink. "Nope. They haven't been here. As you know, I had to go out east to get married, too. Those New York folks wouldn't venture out here for anything. They didn't want nothing to do with this wild country. It's a wonder and a blessing for me she ever made it out here. But Susan was born to live here. I'll tell you that! Her family could never understand it. But then she went and wanted to be buried back in the east. Things are hard to figure sometimes.

"Come to think of it, I just saw one of those new horseless carriages coming down the street. I suspect those things are all over New York City. That should provide some comfort for them when they get to town."

Fran stood up straight and rubbed his whiskers. "They'll replace the horse soon, even here."

"Yeah. Well, that's a future I can do without."

Evinrude finished the glass of whiskey

and poured himself another.

"Those things don't look reliable to me. I don't see how anything will ever come of it."

"Times are changing, Mr. Evinrude. Things never stay the same."

"Fran, remember last summer when they had the grand opening and ball for this place? Lit it up with all those electric lights? At the time, I thought I'd never see the likes of that again. It was something to behold. Now, I'm not so sure. Who knows what they'll come up with next?"

* * *

THE TWO HAD SPENT some time idly chatting about local events and gossip when Colt appeared abruptly in the saloon. He grinned widely and quickly handed Evinrude the telegram he had retrieved. Evinrude read it and then gestured to Fran.

"Get my man here a glass, if you will, Fran. I bet he's thirsty. We don't have to be back at the ranch until tomorrow."

Evinrude turned to Colt. "Colt, my daughter, Janel, will be here soon from the east.

She's coming in on the train. The last time I had correspondence from her, she went on about being involved in the moving picture business—some craziness about wanting to be the Biograph girl or something. I don't have any idea what that is. I don't know what to make of all of it."

Colt was confused. He had never been out of Montana. "From the east, Mr. Evinrude? From the Dakotas?"

"No. Farther east. New York City."

Colt greedily took a drink from the glass of whiskey that had been set in front of him.

"New York City? I guess I heard about that place once or twice. Do you think they do much ranchin' and cowboyin' out there?"

"I doubt it. It's a big city. Lots of people and lots of hurrying around."

Colt's confusion grew. "Why would a ranch gal want to get involved in that kind of mess?"

"She's got stars in her eyes, Colt. She thinks the big city is where the future is and apparently that the moving picture business will sweep across the land."

Colt furrowed his brow. "What the hell is

this moving picture business about? I never heard of such a thing."

Evinrude placed a hand on his chin and said, "From what I understand, they can take a bunch of pictures, move them real fast in front of people, and it looks like something from real life."

"Move them real fast? Do they have folks run across in front of the people carrying a picture? That don't make a lot of sense to me. It seems kind of strange."

Evinrude looked at Colt with exasperation.

"No, for crying out loud. They have a machine that does it. You've never heard of moving pictures?"

Fran joined the conversation. "That's right. They have a machine that shines a light and puts the images up on a screen. They call it a bioscope or something like that. I saw a moving picture show over in Helena. It was called *The Great Train Robbery*. It looked just like real life, but kinda choppy."

Colt pushed his hat back on his head. "They showed a moving picture about a train robbery! What for?"

"For entertainment, son. The people loved it. It was quite a wonder to see."

"Entertainment? People paid to see some folks getting robbed on a train. The world gets stranger all the time. I like to go to a dance or the saloon for my entertainment. Now that I think of it, there's probably some good money in train robbing if a man can stay away from being strung up for it. I can't see somebody paying to see a train get robbed. I'm surprised the law doesn't have something to say about that."

Evinrude and Fran both looked at each other, astonished at Colt's ignorance. Colt didn't notice. He was now lost deep in thought.

The rest of the evening passed uneventfully. A little more whiskey was consumed, along with a fine dinner. Colt and Evinrude retired to their rooms early after stabling the horses; morning would come soon enough, and they needed to return to the ranch.

THE JOURNEY BEGINS

The idea of striking out as an adventurer, like the great Don Quixote, had taken hold in Colt's mind. It occupied his thoughts night and day after his return to the ranch. No more tedious work tending sheep and a few cows. A man of his talents needed to set his path in the world, not wait for excitement to come to him. Colt made a decision. He would quit his ranch life and become a full-time adventurer. Now all he had to do was tell Jim Evinrude that he was quitting. Colt didn't relish the thought of the reaction that might bring from the grizzled J-Bar-T owner, but it had to be done.

What kind of adventurer would he be if he couldn't face a little fear?

* * *

Colt approached Jim Evinrude with trepidation. Evinrude was leaning on the railing of a sheep pen, intently studying the animals inside. Colt steeled himself for the earful he was likely to receive from his boss when he broke the news of his leaving.

When Colt reached the sheep pen, Evinrude looked over at him.

"Good morning, Colt. How are things going?"

Colt looked down and kicked at the dirt before saying, "Pretty good, Mr. Evinrude. I need to talk to you for a minute. I'm fixin' to leave out of here and would like to collect any wages due me before I go."

Evinrude squinted. "Leaving? What the hell for? Don't I pay you good enough?"

Colt continued to look down and fidget. "Yes, sir. You've always paid good wages, and the feed is fine here too. I'm just looking to set out on a different path."

Evinrude's voice rose as he said, "You're

not going over to work on the Bair place, are you?"

Colt, becoming a little more comfortable, looked up at his boss. "Nope. I'm gonna start in on the adventurin' business."

Evinrude recoiled a bit, and his voice rose further. "Adventuring? What in the world, son? A man has to work. Earn a wage. Either that or start his own outfit. The only path in life is hard work and clean living. I've never heard of such a thing!"

Colt straightened up and tried to look as confident as possible. He said firmly, "Well, Mr. Evinrude. I have my mind set on adventurin', and I mean to do it."

Evinrude slowly shook his head, not quite able to believe what he was hearing from the young cowboy. "I don't know what the hell gets into young people these days. I think you come from a decent family, Colt. Your parents had to have raised you right. This adventuring path you want to go down is going to be a short one. I'm not even sure what the hell you mean by adventuring. It's not an occupation that I've ever heard of. Sounds like loafing to me."

After studying Colt from top to bottom,

Evinrude flipped a hand up. "Alright, follow me back to the ranch house, and we'll get things squared up. You're not a prisoner here. You're a grown man; I guess you can make your own decisions."

"Thank you, sir."

The two men left the sheep pen and walked to the ranch house. Evinrude paid Colt his wages, and a little more for good measure. They shook hands, and Colt returned to the bunkhouse to collect his things. After Colt packed up his few possessions, he saddled his buckskin horse and headed out. He didn't say goodbye to his companions, who were scattered about the ranch, working on various tasks. It saddened him a little to leave them without a goodbye, but he was in a good mood overall, looking forward to all the new and exciting adventures that were sure to come his way.

COLT'S first order of business was to locate a place to set up camp. He couldn't go back to the small family ranch. That was not a possibility. He grimaced at the thought of his father learning about his new vocation. He could almost hear him sputtering in indignation, and a light chuckle escaped Colt's lips. An image of his father's stern face crossed his mind, and Colt imagined the old man's body seizing up from shock upon hearing the news of his new life. He chuckled even harder despite himself; his father was not the type to stand for any kind of recklessness.

He had come from a solid, hard-working family. They were never rich, but they also never knew poverty; Colt had never experienced want. But his father was a rigid man who didn't believe that life was meant to be fun, and if any fun or entertainment was allowed, his father doled it out in small portions. Colt's mother never questioned his father, and she was very religious. Colt thought it likely that his mother would feel that the devil himself had taken over her son if he showed up at the home place and announced his intentions. Nope, he was on his own when it came to adventuring.

Colt rode toward Barber, a small stop on the railroad. He knew a spot by the Musselshell River that would make a good campsite, offering cover and some privacy. The site reminded him of a place he used to go with a red-haired girl when he was a boy. In Barber, he could get what supplies he needed without drawing too much attention. He couldn't set up in the Harlowton area. He knew too many people there, and they would start asking questions he didn't want to answer. It wouldn't take long for word to get around that he was no longer working for the J-Bar-T.

He followed a game trail that ran along the railroad tracks until he saw it branch off and turn toward the river. This was the spot. He urged his horse down a small embankment and into the tall grass that lined the trail. The grass brushed against his legs as he rode and soon gave way to a small circular clearing in a stand of cottonwood trees. It was little more than an old cattle wallow, but Colt thought it would work well enough for a camp to start his adventuring. It provided shelter from the elements, and he could always pull some fish from the river to eat. He unsaddled his horse, hobbled it, and began setting up his camp.

After setting up the camp, Colt went over to his saddlebags and retrieved his prized possessions, a collection of pulp magazines filled with stories of the Old West. No one knew he had them. They had been acquired in Harlowton at the general store, and some of them he had possessed since his time living at home. He had successfully hidden them from his parents, and since he had been living on his own, he had hidden them from his workmates.

They were his and his alone, a private world that no one else could access. Colt had read through them many times, never tiring of the stories. In the magazines, the world existed the way Colt thought things should be in life. A life unrestrained by boredom and tedious work. One of excitement and constant adventure. Did Kit Carson and Jesse James answer to anyone? Did they toil day after day in the scorching sun or the cold, relentless wind for meager wages and an old bed in the corner of a bunkhouse? No, sir. They made their way in life with no one telling them what to do. These were men of renown and fame. Not some poor cowboy working on a sheep ranch. Why couldn't Colt do the same thing? Live a life that way. Had times changed that much? Hearing about

Don Quixote had settled the matter for him. It was his destiny to go this route, and he would do it come hell or high water. He smiled contentedly as he sat down to delve into one of his treasures.

* * *

THE DAY PASSED by lazily as Colt read his magazines and slept. Soon it was evening, and the sun was just about to drop below the horizon. Colt gathered up whatever wood he could scrounge and built a fire. Meager supplies were pulled from his saddlebags, and a meal was prepared. A nice fat trout from the river would have been an excellent complement to the meal. There was just one problem. Colt had forgotten to bring along anything that could be used for fishing. Oh well, he would get some supplies in Barber. Colt had little money, but that was no problem. He was sure to get more once he was an established adventurer.

Colt sat around the fire for a while, doing nothing but dreaming of the glory and fame that was soon to come his way. Thirsty for something more than water, he grabbed a bottle of whiskey. He frowned as he looked at the bottle. There was only a quarter left. Colt pulled the cork and took a slow drink. Darkness had arrived, and his horse moved closer to the fire, grazing peacefully, moving in and out of the light. Colt began to talk to the animal.

"I need to get started on this adventurin' real quick, old boy. You and me are running a little low on supplies. What to do? Hey, I know what we'll do. We'll rob us a train. That oughta bring in some good money. Jesse James made his living doing it. Why not me? They're making moving pictures of folks robbing trains these days. I might even get famous. Maybe they might even make a moving picture of me doing it. You never know, do you?"

The horse continued grazing peacefully, and since the animal offered no protest to his plan, Colt continued.

"Trains are running up and down the tracks all the time round here. Trains carrying folks from the east who got money and valuable things. Rich folks. They don't need all that money. Why not donate a little to a man trying to get started in a new venture?

Yep, that's what we're gonna do, Buck. In fact, I'm thinking there's probably a train coming through tomorrow morning sometime."

The horse stopped eating, raised its head, looked at Colt for a moment, and then went back to its meal.

"How are we going to do it? It can't be that hard, can it? Jesse used to put stuff up on the tracks and block the train, so it had to stop. Let's do that. That should work. We'll haul up some trees and stuff, put it on the tracks and block the train. Then when they stop, we'll stick the damn thing up. They won't know what hit'em!"

Colt grinned and clapped his hands, proud of his plan. Then the grin turned to a grimace.

"Wait, I forgot something. A fella robbing trains needs a name. I can't just say my name. That would be dumb as hell. They'd have me strung up in a day or two. Can't be having that. Hmm ... I got it! The Cottonwood Kid! That's what it'll be. Dang, Buck. I really think we're on to something here. I can't wait to get started. Let's grab a little sleep before the adventurin' begins tomorrow."

Colt's grin returned, and he stared at his

horse; the buckskin stared back. Colt took that as validation, and as far as he was concerned, his outlaw name was set in stone.

"I'm glad you like my outlaw name, Buck. From now on, don't forget to call me the Cottonwood Kid. Folks are gonna be hearing that name for a long time."

Colt took one more drink of whiskey from the bottle, corked it, and pulled a blanket over his body. He was soon asleep.

THE GREAT HARLOWTON
TRAIN ROBBERY

*C*olt groggily awoke and sat up, his eyes adjusting to the bright sunlight already filtering through the trees. He had slept in much later than usual, and he cursed himself for his negligence. If he didn't get moving, he'd miss the train and all his plans would be dashed. This wasn't the way he had intended to start off his new adventuring business.

He slowly rose and made his way to the river, stopping to splash some cold water on his face before filling up a canteen with the clear liquid. Back at camp, he measured out as much coffee as he could spare into a tin pot and set it over a quickly built fire. The smell of the brewing coffee filled the air, but the rationed amount wasn't nearly enough for Colt to feel truly refreshed. Hardtack, softened from a soak in the coffee, served as an unsatisfactory breakfast. Still, excitement flowed like a river through Colt's body. Today was going to be big if he could make it in time for the train.

After finishing breakfast, Colt extinguished the remaining embers of the fire by kicking dirt on them and applying the coup de grâce with the last of the coffee. The embers sizzled and smoked as they reached the end of their life. He stretched his arms high above his head and yawned, ridding the last of the sleepiness from his body.

After packing up his gear, he retrieved his horse. He gave his trusty partner an affectionate pat on the neck as he led the animal over to the saddle and gear. Colt bent down and picked up the saddle and saddle blanket, swiftly hoisting them onto the horse's back, humming a tune as he cinched the saddle up tight. In no time, the newly minted train robber was ready to go. He addressed his partner in crime, a little embarrassed that things were off to a slow start.

"Sorry about this, old pal. Buck, we need to get moving. I must've been tired to have slept so long. I hope we didn't miss that train. We need to get up the tracks toward Barber a little. That's where we'll waylay it. We won't be coming back here today, but we'll be back sometime soon. I reckon we'll be on the scout for a bit after adventurin' on that train. We don't have folks who'll take us in like Jesse James had. Jesse had it good in that respect. Well, let's skedaddle out of here."

Colt jumped into the saddle and tightened his grip on the reins as he spurred his horse into action. The rhythmic pounding of hooves against the ground was like music as he went up the trail, and Colt's heart beat a little faster in anticipation of what the day might bring. He traveled quickly until he reached a point that he judged to be about half the distance between his camp and Barber. To the south of the tracks, he noted some rough country that would make a good escape route. Colt nodded his head in approval. This would be the spot. He stopped his horse and slid out of the saddle, landing lightly on the ground.

"This looks good. We can escape out of

here to the south in those breaks. We'll be long gone before any law can catch us. I hope the loot we get isn't too heavy. That'll slow us down. That's a good problem to have, though. We'll have to find a place to stash it out here in the hills. One we can remember easily. That'd be something if we got a bunch of loot and forgot where we put it. Can't let that happen. Let's see about getting some trees up on the tracks."

He looked around. There were plenty of fallen trees and detritus lying around off the trail. However, most of it was lying about in a tangled mess. That didn't deter the would-be train robber, and he began trying to separate the larger fallen trees from the general mess. It didn't work. He could move nothing of consequence up to the tracks.

Sweating heavily from the exertion, Colt stopped working to rest. At that moment, he heard a whistle and saw smoke in the distance.

"The train's coming! I don't have time for any more of this tree stuff. What am I going to do? I know. I'll tie my bandana on a stick and try to flag'em down. Maybe they'll stop. Wait! I got an idea! Buck, I'll put you up in the middle of the tracks with me. They'll have to stop. They wouldn't run over a horse! Would they? Don't worry, Buck. You'll be fine. I promise."

Colt tied his bandana on the end of a stick and led his horse onto the railroad tracks. He then began frantically waving the stick. This action startled the horse, and the animal moved skittishly off the tracks. Colt held on tight to the reins, regained control of the horse, and led Buck back into position. He petted Buck softly, trying to calm him.

"Easy, boy. Easy. Nothing bad is gonna happen. We need to get this train stopped."

Buck calmed down, and Colt resumed waving the stick; the bandana fluttering wildly in the air. The sound of the train whistle grew louder and louder as the great metal beast bore down on them. Closer and closer it came, then suddenly, the piercing screech of brakes filled the air, drowning out all other sounds. Colt held his ground, and the train shuddered to a stop, the locomotive halting only fifty feet away from Colt and his trusty steed.

Strangely, the horse was unaffected by the screeching stop of the train. The horse's behavior perplexed Colt; he fully expected Buck to bolt because of the loud screeching sound. Shaking his head, he softly said, "That's peculiar." Horses were hard to figure sometimes. Colt wrapped the reins loosely around the saddle horn and let the animal go. He wasn't worried about the horse straying too far. It never did, and a little whistle would bring Buck running to him. He waited for someone to appear.

* * *

THE GRIMY FACE of the driver materialized out of the side of the locomotive, waving an equally grimy arm. He looked angry.

"What the hell is the meaning of this? Why'd you stop the train like that? I could have killed you and that buckskin. It was a dumb thing to do. Is there some kind of emergency?"

Colt suddenly realized the man could see his face. He quickly grabbed the bandana off the end of the stick, hastily tied it around his neck, and slid it over his nose. The answer to the driver's questions came as a pistol aimed directly at the driver's head, and a simple statement.

"Listen up. I'm fixin' to rob this train."

The driver was astonished. "Robbing the train? Where's the rest of the gang? I bet they're in the bushes off the tracks."

Colt replied pleasantly, "Nope. This is a one-man train robbery, fella. Now, don't do something stupid that might get you shot."

The driver ducked his head back inside the locomotive and informed the rest of the crew of the situation.

The conductor had also looked down the tracks and saw the lone man standing in front of the locomotive. He walked quickly alongside the train toward Colt. His first thought was not that of a train robbery. Like the driver, he also thought someone had stopped the train for an emergency. As he got closer, he saw that the man standing in the tracks had a bandana over his face. Still, he didn't think of a robbery. What kind of fool would try to rob a train by himself? He was mad and stopped a few feet in front of Colt, standing rigidly with his hands on his hips.

The conductor glared at Colt and said, "Is this some kind of prank, or is there an emergency? You damn cowboys are always up to these kinds of shenanigans. The train robbing days are long past. You just bought yourself a heap of trouble, mister."

Startled by the appearance of the conductor, Colt took a step back, but quickly regained his composure and tried to look as intimidating as possible. "No, sir! This isn't a joke at all. Now get your hands up, or you'll learn what it's like to mess with the Cottonwood Kid."

The conductor was armed with a small pistol, but in his anger and disbelief, he had failed to draw the weapon as he approached Colt. Now, suddenly realizing that a robbery was really happening, he tried to retrieve the weapon, fumbling with it.

Whatever other shortcomings Colt may have possessed, he was a fine shot with his pistol, fast too. He immediately responded with a shot and hit the conductor in the shoulder. The conductor fell to the ground, dropping his pistol and clutching his injured shoulder. Colt had hit exactly where he had aimed. There was no need to be killing folks if it could be avoided.

Colt grinned under the bandana, proud of

his quick shot. "That was a poor move, mister. Things didn't have to go that way. Now, get to your feet and take me to the diner car. This train robbing business is making me kinda hungry."

At the sound of the shot, more heads appeared, peering out of windows, and more of the train crew emerged to determine the nature of the commotion.

Colt yelled out, "Look here, everybody! I'm the Cottonwood Kid, and I'm robbing this train! Anyone who wants to join in the fun and not get shot better head for the diner. If you're already there, stay put."

This declaration had its intended effect, and word was passed along that everyone was to move to the dining car. Those not already relaxing in the diner shuffled along in that direction, whispering among themselves, both confused and excited.

Colt was about to head toward the dining car when a thought flitted across his mind. He barked, "Wait a second! I need you train workers to uncouple the locomotive and move it forward a bit. I don't want you takin' off with me to Harlowton before I finish my adventurin'. Come along! Be quick about it!"

Firing a couple of shots in the air, Colt took a crouched stance and looked wildly around. A menacing outlaw if there ever was one. Colt was genuinely enjoying himself, and he chuckled with glee as the driver and brakeman reluctantly came forward to assist him.

He pointed his pistol at them. "See about your business, gentlemen. Get that locomotive uncoupled."

The brakeman uncoupled the locomotive, and the driver eased it forward. Suddenly, a loud voice came from the locomotive. "I'm heading for Harlowton! I'll be back with the law!" The engine on the locomotive slowly opened up, the great beast hissing and churning as it gained speed. It soon disappeared up the tracks, leaving a momentary silence in its wake.

Colt laughed. "A lot of good that'll do him. I'll be finished robbing this train and on my way before any law gets here. Besides, I'm a match for any two-bit lawman around here."

He took a deep breath and said loudly, "Alright, everybody! Keep moving to the diner. There's business that needs tending."

* * *

INSIDE THE PARLOR CAR, a young woman pulled her head back inside and exclaimed, "Aunt Mary, we're being held up!"

In response, an older woman in a fine dress put her hands to her face. "Oh, it can't be true! Is it natives on the rampage? What's going to happen to us?"

The young woman rolled her eyes and laughed. "It's not natives, Auntie. It looks like one man. He seems to mean business. This is all very exciting. You don't get a hold-up on a train ride every day!"

Sitting across from them, the young woman's cousin frowned and said, "I'll take care of this brute. He'll learn not to mess with a New Yorker."

Dalton was an athletic young man with jet-black hair. He moved about the world with an exaggerated confidence, and with what appeared to be a permanent smirk, as though he knew a secret that no one else would ever know. His confidence came from his training as a boxer, although his competition had been limited and carefully curated. It was a house built on a foundation of sand.

His mother did not support his endeavors as a boxer, believing it was not befitting a young man of his social standing.

Aunt Mary was now anxious, and her son's declaration did nothing to quell that feeling. Her eyes darted all around like agitated bees. Her gaunt body was rigid in her seat, and her thin fingers danced like spiders across her lap. A sea of gray hair was done up tightly on her head, and her cheeks and lips were pale, though plump compared to the rest of her face. Large eyes blinked rapidly beneath spectacles.

"I don't like this one bit. You never know what ruffians like that mean to do to respectable women of our standing."

The young woman laughed even harder. "I suspect he means to relieve us of our valuables. As for you, Dalton, you'll do nothing. The man is armed, and you aren't. This isn't New York City. You're likely to be killed if you mess with him."

Amid the excitement, a man entered the parlor car and informed the group that the bandit had ordered everyone into the diner. The group dutifully gathered themselves and began their trek.

* * *

THE PASSENGERS and crew of the train had fully assembled in the dining car. They were over their initial alarm, and curiosity replaced their fear. They waited to see what the bandit would do next, and the air of the crowded train car was heavy with anticipation.

Although the passengers would have been able to overpower the lone robber easily, had they possessed sufficient courage, no resistance appeared. Human nature and the desire for self-preservation being what it is, passivity settled in among the assembled crowd. Most were more than willing to turn over their valuables.

Colt entered the dining car with authority, running his hand over polished brass and burnished wood. He had never seen such a sight. His life had mostly been one of sensible restraint. Luxuries were few. Now, he stood in a place designed specifically for comfort and luxury. It mesmerized him, and he looked around in amazement.

He couldn't help but be envious as he

nodded in admiration. "So, this is how rich folks live!"

The clinking of a cup being set firmly on a hard surface broke Colt's trance. His eyes suddenly snapped back into focus, bringing him out of his daze. After all, there was a train robbery that needed attending. He aimed his pistol at the assembled passengers, and the group recoiled in fear. Colt took a crouched stance, as though he were ready to fire at any moment.

"Listen up, people. Don't be getting any crazy ideas, and you'll all make it through this. I'm the Cottonwood Kid. I come out of Wyoming. Rode with Tom Horn for a while. I've been at this business for a long time and seen every dirty trick you might play on me. Don't try anything. My trigger finger is getting mighty itchy."

An old man shouted from the back of the diner. "I was down in Cheyenne when Horn stood trial in 1902. They hung him in 1903. I don't remember hearing anything about a Cottonwood Kid riding with him. I thought Horn worked alone."

Colt peered at the back of the diner. He pointed his pistol in that direction like he was pointing a finger and said, "You calling me a liar, mister? I'll fill you full of lead right now. Be quiet, you hear. I'm the one who's going to do the talking round this place."

He heard the giggle of a woman coming from the crowd.

Colt responded defiantly to the giggle. "What?! Who's that laughing? It's mighty rude and foolish to be laughing at a man holding all the cards."

Janel Evinrude pushed through to the front of the group. She couldn't resist getting a good look at the train robber. Her view from the parlor car hadn't been very good, and she had been busy dealing with her relatives. Janel sized Colt up quickly once she saw him up close.

This character is just a plain cowboy masquerading as a bandit. He strikes quite a figure, though. He might even be handsome if he took that bandana off his face. This is wonderful. What excitement! He'd make a great cowboy in the moving pictures. Tall, fit. It looks like he has green eyes. Yes, they are green. I love green eyes in a man!

Janel beamed a bright smile at Colt. Her long, blonde hair shone like a golden halo around her soft, oval face. It made her bright blue eyes seem like jewels in a mine. Janel's glowing smile brightened the room, immediately freezing Colt. She was so pretty that he stared at her in stunned silence for a few seconds. Then, recovering his senses, his eyes began studying her curvy body. Ever the gentleman, at least in his mind, he tipped his hat.

"Good day, miss. It's a pleasure to meet you. I'll try to get this robbing business done pretty quickly so as not to disturb you too much. An outlaw I am, but my folks raised me proper. I don't want to be causing too much distress to a young lady."

Janel smirked and performed an exaggerated curtsy. "That's mighty kind of you. It's nice to meet you too, sir. I'm Janel Evinrude and my father is Jim Evinrude. He runs a big spread in these parts, a ranch called the J-Bar-T. Maybe you've heard of it. If this train doesn't show up in Harlowton on time, he's likely to come looking for me. I will say, though, this train robbing is exciting."

This information unnerved Colt for a moment and he stammered, "Well … Uh … No, miss. I've never heard of the place. Like I said,

I come out of Wyoming. I don't know anything about the J-Bar-T."

Janel smiled as brightly as ever, but now a little malice crept into her voice. "It's just as well. Once folks find out you've robbed this train, they'll be a bunch of them out to hang you, including my father and his men. It's better for you if you aren't known around these parts. You might have a chance of getting away, but I'm thinking your odds aren't good."

Colt became defiant again. He was the Cottonwood Kid! The one in charge of this situation. He said dismissively, "Hang me? Not a chance. They'll have to catch me first, and I can tell you, miss, that ain't gonna happen. I'll sure as hell get away, whether I'm known in these parts or not. But I'm telling you, I bet a lot of folks have heard of the Cottonwood Kid."

A smell wafted through the air, and Colt suddenly changed the subject.

"Say, I smell something good. This whole business has made me hungry. I bet there is some pretty fine grub on this train. Where's that conductor I shot in the shoulder? Get up here quick, fella."

The conductor shuffled to the front. He looked peaked and sullen; sweat dotted his forehead. He clutched at his wounded shoulder as though he might collapse at any moment. However, inside, he was steaming mad at Colt. But fear kept him from any outward expression of anger.

Colt gazed at the conductor, his eyes glowing with disgust. "What's your problem, fella? You're the one who pulled a gun on me first. What was I supposed to do? Let you shoot me? You're lucky to have gone up against the Cottonwood Kid and lived. It looks like you just have a flesh wound. Show a little grit." He waved his pistol in a small circle. "Now, have your attendants rustle up some grub for everyone here. Folks need to eat, and damn, I'm hungry. Get with it! That locomotive will be back with the law before too long. I need a little head start on them."

The conductor dutifully summoned the kitchen attendants, and they went to work on setting up the diner for a meal. The attendants decided they would lay a buffet out instead of taking individual orders; it would save time. Preparation began in earnest.

The mood in the dining car changed.

Now, with a few exceptions, most people seemed to enjoy themselves and no longer saw the event as dangerous. Nothing would have seemed out of the ordinary if an outsider had entered the diner at that moment. They would have witnessed calm conversation, laughter, and general mingling among the passengers. The only thing that would have seemed out of place would have been one strange-looking cowboy with a bandana over his face seated at a front table, his pistol resting on it. His manner resembling that of a feudal lord surveying his subjects.

It didn't take long for the buffet to be laid out, and the passengers began eating like it was their last meal. Janel Evinrude brought Colt a plate of food served with a half-smile. Colt couldn't take his eyes off her. Not only was he very attracted to her, but he was sure she knew he was not an outlaw. She, of all the people on the train, knew his true self. Knew that he hadn't ridden with Tom Horn or any outlaw, that he was just a cowboy out robbing a train for the first time. The fact that Janel had pegged him for what he really was didn't bother him at all.

After eating a large plate of food, comically raising the bandana each time to take a bite, Colt started to feel a little antsy. The locomotive had left for Harlowton some time ago, and certainly it would be back with people who were hostile to his adventuring. It was time to go.

Colt stood up and announced to the passengers, "Folks, it's time for me to say good-bye. It's been a pleasure robbing this train and spending time with you, but I reckon the law is on its way back here. A lawman won't see things the same way we all do."

A man stood on the tips of his toes, waved his hand rapidly and said, "Kid! You haven't really robbed us. You haven't taken any loot. Most train robbers like to get a little stash before they head out."

The crowd laughed and Colt laughed with them, embarrassed that he had forgotten that small, but important fact. "Good grief! You're right. I almost forgot to collect loot from you fine folks. And I forgot to bring a bag with me. Just put your money and coins in that man's hat and pass it to me."

Colt pointed to a man wearing a bowler hat. The man removed his hat, put a few coins in it, and passed it to the next person.

When everyone had donated sufficiently to the hat, a passenger meekly handed it to Colt. Of course, the money donated to the hat was nowhere near the amount of cash actually possessed by those on the train. But the genial nature of the bandit spurred some generosity in those donating to the cause of the Cottonwood Kid.

Looking in the hat, Colt was pleased by what he saw. He took the money and stuffed it in his pockets, then tossed the hat back to its owner. "This will do just fine. It'll pay for a good time somewhere. I thank y'all kindly. Well, I'm off."

He tipped his hat, winked at Janel, and quickly left the dining car. Colt walked up to the front of the train. Buck was grazing peacefully off the side of the tracks, and he retrieved the horse without incident. Leaping into the saddle, he rode up the hills to the south of the tracks.

When he reached the crest, Colt turned his horse back to face the train. Many people had disembarked to see the departure of the desperado, while others looked out the windows of the dining car. Colt took off his hat and waved it to the onlookers, then spun the horse and galloped out of sight.

Once Colt was out of sight, Dalton turned to Janel and said, "That criminal is lucky I didn't box his ears, take his pistol from him, and arrest him."

Janel tilted her head slightly forward and raised an eyebrow. "You would have done no such thing, Dalton, and you know it. Just feel lucky that you got to see an honest-to-goodness train robbery. That Cottonwood Kid sure was quite a character. Dreamy, really. Those nice green eyes. I won't forget them. He needs to be in the moving pictures with me."

* * *

THE LOCOMOTIVE EVENTUALLY ARRIVED BACK AT the train. Colt was long gone, and the passengers were milling about, talking about the day's events, finishing what was left of the buffet.

With the locomotive came the local sheriff, Jack Sedgwick. Sedgwick was a sensible, even-tempered man, not prone to violence but not afraid of it either. He was a man of imposing size. Size that made his very presence potent. He wasn't overly muscled, but his strength was clear in his sure manner. When he walked, it was slow and deliberate. A kind of shuffle, with his hands cutting across his body as he traveled.

He began questioning the passengers somewhat disinterestedly. The locomotive driver had given him a description of the bandit, but it was too vague to be of any value. He didn't believe the passengers would add anything that would be useful.

Sedgwick was right, little of value was learned from the passengers. They agreed the bandit had been a lanky man who called himself the Cottonwood Kid. He claimed to have come from Wyoming and been an experienced outlaw. He had not been overly violent for his occupation and appeared somewhat dull-witted. Only Janel Evinrude could offer any helpful information.

"Well, Sheriff Sedgwick, I think he was just a dumb cowboy acting like a desperado. He had the stance and dress of a cowhand, that's for sure. I've seen plenty of them in my life. He didn't know what he was doing, so he couldn't have been experienced. Who lingers about during a train robbery and has a meal with the people he's robbing? He didn't even get away with much money. It was like what people put in the offering plate at a Sunday service. He had nice green eyes. I'd recognize those eyes anywhere now. I think he was a young man. He had the attitude of one."

"Thank you, Miss Evinrude. We'll get into Harlowton as soon as we can. Your father will be eager to see you."

Janel was still excited by the robbery, and the words spilled out of her rapidly as she said, "Are you going to send out a posse and trackers? Run him to ground?"

The sheriff shook his head. "No, there's no need for that right now. I'll put out some feelers around the area. I think this character is probably local. No experienced bandit would travel alone to rob a train far from his home. Most experienced men wouldn't try to rob a train alone, period. Unless they were really desperate, and this character certainly wasn't acting desperate."

Sedgwick paused, scratched his temple, and contemplated the situation. Then he continued, "I've never heard a word about anyone calling himself the Cottonwood Kid.

Most of the notorious men are dead now, in jail somewhere or keeping a low profile. The old days are fading away. That doesn't mean that new criminals don't pop up all the time. It just means this Cottonwood Kid isn't one of the already notorious ones. He kinda strikes me as a fool. I agree, he is a young local cowboy out on some lark."

Janel pointed a finger to the hills where Colt was last seen. "He took off into those hills, Sheriff Sedgwick."

Staring at the hills, Sedgwick said slowly, "Not much out in those hills. At some point, he'll have to come back to civilization for supplies and such. A man like him will probably also be looking for some entertainment. Somebody will hear something useful. Let's get this locomotive hitched back up and be on our way."

BACK IN HARLOWTON

The Harlowton train station was alight with eager and anxious faces. A large crowd had gathered awaiting the passengers in what the *Harlowton News* would soon refer to in headlines as The Great Harlowton Train Robbery, even though the event took place closer to Barber. Amid the carnival-like atmosphere, Jim Evinrude stood vigil, tensely waiting for his daughter. Other than the news that a bandit had robbed the Milwaukee, no one in Harlowton had any clue as to the fate of the passengers. Rumors swirled like the dust kicked up by the children running around the station. The crowd expected the passengers would appear as bedraggled survivors, with tattered clothes and haunted eyes.

There was palpable disappointment among the crowd when the train arrived. What disembarked from the train were jovial, excited people ready to share their story, not scarred remnants of a mortal struggle. Evinrude breathed a sigh of relief at the sight of the first passengers who disembarked; they looked to be in good spirits and unharmed. He moved back and forth from foot to foot as he waited for Janel to get off the train. When she appeared, he pushed his way through the crowd and greeted her with a hug.

"My goodness, Janel. I'm happy to see you. I was worried sick. What happened out there? Was it a gang that robbed the train?"

Janel stepped back from her father, grinning from ear to ear. "We're all fine, Dad. It was all good fun. It was just a lone robber, and we sat down to a fine buffet with him before he took off into the hills."

"A buffet? What in the world are you talking about?"

"Yes, a buffet. The robber seemed to be a dumb cowboy. I would say that the whole thing was a joke, except for the fact that he put a bullet in the conductor."

"Is the conductor still alive?"

"He's fine. A wound to the shoulder. I believe he'll live. The train robbing added fun to an otherwise dreary trip. I'm really OK. There's nothing to be worried about."

Evinrude relaxed, now fully convinced his daughter was unaffected by the ordeal. "I'm glad you're in such fine spirits after experiencing something like that. It's quite a homecoming. Everybody is excited to see you back on the ranch, but they're worried you might have changed a lot after being in the big city for so long."

Janel scoffed at the notion that she had changed. "They don't need to worry. I'm still a Montana girl at heart. I haven't changed much at all."

Jim looked over Janel's shoulder and saw Mary and Dalton standing behind her. Mary had never been happy about the fact that her sister had married a sheep rancher from Montana, and it showed in the scowl that she directed at Jim. Mary fully believed that her sister would still be alive had she not taken up residence in such a wild, uncivilized place. As for Dalton, he had been little more than a boy the last time Jim had seen him, and Jim nodded in approval at the young man now standing there. He greeted Mary first.

"Mary, how are you? Some time has passed since we last saw each other. Did you enjoy the trip?"

Mary continued to scowl at Jim, and replied curtly, "I'm as good as I can be, considering a ruffian just robbed me. The people in these wild lands seem to be barbaric. They don't rob trains like this back east. It makes me nervous being so far from civilization, but I came on this trip for Janel's sake. She needed an escort."

"Mary, you know I'll make you whole if the bandit took anything from you."

"He got nothing from me, the scoundrel. However, I was worried about protecting my virtue and your daughter's. Who knows what a man like that will try?" She straightened her dress and shuddered at the thought.

Jim shifted uneasily and looked quickly to Dalton. "I see ... OK, Dalton, how are you, son? You look like a grown man now." He stepped forward and shook Dalton's hand.

"I'm doing well, Mr. Evinrude. Had I

armed myself, I would've given that bandit something to think about right on the spot."

"I bet you would've, son. There's no doubt in my mind. Let me get someone to see about the luggage, and we'll head up to the Graves. We'll stay overnight and head out to the ranch tomorrow. It's been a big day, and I'm sure everyone could use a little rest. Is anyone opposed to walking? The hotel is just up the hill, and the walk will be nice."

Mary raised a hand in protest. "I don't know if I'm up to walking anywhere. Isn't there a carriage that can be called for a ride?"

Janel quickly came to the aid of her father. "Oh, come on, Aunt Mary! A little walking will do you good. It'll work up an appetite for the food at the Graves. You'll love it. It's just up the hill a bit."

Mary pursed her lips and relented to Janel's goading. "Alright, I'll do it if you insist, Janel. But it doesn't seem very ladylike. I guess that's what you people do out here."

Jim clapped his hands together. "Good, it's agreed. Let me get the luggage sorted out, and we'll get crackin' on our walk. Oh, by the way, we have one heck of a party planned for you all when we get back to the ranch. It'll take a few days to get everything ready, but it will be a doozy."

* * *

SHERIFF SEDGWICK SAT in a chair in his office, looking at a copy of the wanted posters he had just received from the printers at the *Harlowton News*. Sedgwick didn't believe the posters were of any value, but he needed to appear to be doing something while he got a handle on the situation.

He agreed with Janel's idea that a local cowboy had been the train robber. It seemed to Sedgwick that the robbery had to have been some kind of joke. It wouldn't be outside the range of possibilities for a young man to carry out such a foolish thing in the name of acting out a Wild West fantasy, but the joke was likely to be on the train robber in the end. He had shot an employee of the railroad and disrupted their train. The Milwaukee people wouldn't look kindly upon those actions, and Sedgwick knew that a railroad detective would soon appear in Harlowton. Whoever this desperado was, he was likely to see the inside of a jail cell for quite some time. The railroad would demand their pound of flesh.

* * *

IT WASN'T long before a railroad detective arrived in Sedgwick's office in the form of Stanton McCloskey. McCloskey was a short, bald, slightly pudgy man, and was not what one would expect to see in a railroad detective. But he was not a man to be trifled with in any manner. He was an expert with a pistol and had experience to back it up. In addition, Stanton was a man of rigid countenance and beliefs. Once a plan took hold of his mind, it was very difficult to divert him from carrying it out. McCloskey rubbed people the wrong way, and as a result, he had very few friends. He was a perfect railroad detective.

McCloskey walked up to Sedgwick's desk without comment and picked up one of the wanted posters. He gazed at the poster for a few moments, then looked at Sedgwick.

Without even offering so much as a hello, he said, "McCloskey's the name. I'm here to help you investigate the recent train robbery in your area. Frankly, I would've had this wanted poster done differently. There's not much information, and one hundred dollars may be excessive for a reward."

Sedgwick cringed, knowing he had no choice but to work with the man. The Milwaukee Railroad had too much pull in the area, and the emissaries of the railroad could not be easily dismissed.

"Well, Mr. McCloskey, we do things differently around here. Anyway, there isn't much information to go on at this point. I trust you have secured lodging."

McCloskey's manner didn't change at all. He spoke to Sedgwick as though he were addressing an employee. "What have you done so far to apprehend the train robber? Have you sent out trackers?"

Sedgwick leaned back in his chair, trying to look relaxed and indifferent to McCloskey's rude behavior. "No, I sure haven't. I don't think there's any need at this point. I think this train robber is someone local in the area. He headed south after the incident, but I think he'll probably stick around this area. I reckon he'll be in a saloon in Harlowton soon enough."

McCloskey wasn't buying this theory, and

he became even more condescending in his tone. "I don't know if I agree with how you're going about this, Sedgwick. You should've tried to run him down immediately. We need to get out and question all the locals if you think he is from around here. Lean on them to give us some information. Proper police work is required in a situation like this."

That was enough! Sedgwick was now angry, and his voice boomed in the small room. "Listen up, McCloskey! You may get away with that in some big city, but you can't just run around here like a bull in a china shop. People will not tolerate it, and you won't get any information of value. In fact, the opposite may occur. I've got people around here in the saloons and such. They hear things. I think some fool of a cowboy did this for whatever reason. He'll be looking for attention and head into a town at some point."

McCloskey shot back, "The bandit injured a railroad employee and robbed the train! We can't just sit around and do nothing. The law's been broken. I intend to go out to the site of the robbery and look for clues."

Sedgwick sat up straight in his chair and pointed a finger at the railroad detective.

"You go right ahead, although you won't find much. If he's not holed up on some ranch around here, he might've circled back and is hiding down along the Musselshell somewhere. It's as good a place as any to hide in these parts. Or he might've headed up into the mountains. Or he might hide out in one of the hundreds of little coulees out in the hills. Could be anywhere around here, and he knows the country a hell of a lot better than you!"

He ran his hand through his hair, trying to calm himself. "But I know one thing about young cowboys. They get bored easy and are always looking for entertainment. This fellow will turn up in a saloon, do a little drinking and run his mouth. That much, I'm sure about. If you want to ride around the hills and get some fresh air, feel free to do so. But if you harass folks around here, things will probably turn south for you, Milwaukee man or not."

The sheriff's anger didn't faze McCloskey, and the railroad detective took on an air of superiority. "Thank you for your theories, Sedgwick, but I'm still going to look around.

It's called due diligence in my line of work, and it has to be done."

Sedgwick waved McCloskey away, like a pesky fly, and said, "OK, McCloskey. Have at it. Let me know what you find out."

McCloskey nodded to the sheriff and left. As McCloskey closed the door, Sedgwick gave him a little wave goodbye.

After the railroad detective's departure, Sedgwick locked up his office and walked across the street to the Oasis Saloon for a drink. Dealing with the detective had brought on a powerful thirst. He feared that if he had to interact with McCloskey for too long, he might turn into a full-blown drunkard. Deep in thought, Sedgwick sat down at a table, paying no attention to anyone in the saloon.

I can't let this matter go on too long. People will expect something to be done. They expect law and order now. That damn McCloskey is going to hound me to no end. It's been a long time since something like a train robbery has happened in the area. This job has been pretty easy up to now. Nothing too serious to deal with. Mainly just a drunk here and there and once in a while, real trouble needs to be sorted out. If I play my cards right, this situation might turn out well for me. I will be the man who took down the desperado of The Great Harlowton Train Robbery. Folks won't forget that.

As he pondered these things, Sedgwick didn't notice a tall young cowboy with green eyes standing at the end of the bar talking to the bartender.

* * *

COLT'S FACE lit up in response to the news he had just received. "You don't say! There's going to be a big shindig at the J-Bar-T for Jim Evinrude's daughter? When?"

The bartender gave Colt an amused look and slid another shot of whiskey over to the young man. "Sure is. They say it's this coming Saturday night. Evinrude has invited all the important folk. Should be quite a party."

Colt gulped the shot of whiskey and let out a satisfied exhale. He took a moment to savor the burn on his tongue and the warmth the liquid brought as it worked its way to his stomach. Sated, he looked up at the stamped tin roof of the saloon, as though studying it, and said, "Hmm ... I used to work for that outfit. I think I left on good terms. They wouldn't run me off the place. Well, I better get going. I got places to be. You have a good day, barkeep."

He tapped the bar with his fingers and made for the saloon door with haste. Sheriff Sedgwick never looked up as Colt stepped out into the afternoon sun.

MANUEL VACA

*T*he year was 1879, and George Parrott and his gang of four men occupied a corner of a saloon in Milestown, Montana Territory. The small community would someday be known as Miles City, but for now, it was a bustling, chaotic place of rough people who catered to nearby Fort Keogh.

The men had been careful to keep their voices low, their words spoken with no more energy than that of a whisper. This was not secrecy, exactly, but a need for caution. Parrott had called them to the saloon to discuss business, to decide on the details of a plan that might bring them great riches. Each of the men had his own opinion as to what should be done, but they all knew it would be Parrott who would make the final decision. As they discussed details, the air in the saloon seemed to thicken, the smell of whiskey and cigar smoke mingling with the tension.

Parrott's eyes were lit up with excitement as the discussion continued. He had gotten word that a wealthy merchant in town, Morris Cahn, would be traveling east in two days with a large amount of money to purchase goods. There was one drawback: Cahn would travel with soldiers from Fort Keogh, who were also going east to collect the army payroll. But Parrott was undaunted. The prospect of a huge haul from robbing Cahn outweighing the risks involved in the endeavor.

Looking around the table at his men, Parrott narrowed his eyes, leaned forward and said, "Boys, we're onto something big. Real big. We have to knock this bastard off. It'll make us rich. We all know Cahn is going to be traveling with soldiers. Yes, that is a bit of a problem, as you all have pointed out. I still say we try it. We'll shadow them till they get down to the breaks by Joubert's Landing. Then make our move if it's possible."

The outlaw's face hardened. Shifting in his chair, he asked, "Is everybody in?"

Parrott took a deep breath and looked pointedly at each member of the group, waiting for any objections. Not that it mattered. Once Parrott asked if everybody was in, there was no backing out of the deal. That needed to be done well before Parrott asked the question. The prospect of easy money had them all nodding their approval, including the youngest among them, Manuel Garcia.

Parrott's eyes rested on him, and he said, "Manuel, I want you to round up some good mounts and get Smitty to stable them at his ranch. We'll switch out our horses there when we've finished the job. Alright?"

Manuel nodded confidently. "Yes, sir, that won't be a problem."

Parrott flashed the group a grin as he clapped his hands together. "Alright then, have some fun while you can. We'll be riding soon enough!"

He got up and headed for the faro table, whistling loudly as he went. On his way, Parrott grabbed a young sporting lady and twirled her around twice before continuing. Arriving at the table, he plunked down in a chair and slapped a large amount of money on the table. He looked around with a big grin and said, "Boys, let's get to gambling."

* * *

ON THE DAY of the robbery, everyone was antsy. The minutes before a job were always tense, but today was different. The men didn't relish the thought of being outgunned in any situation. Now they faced the prospect of far more firepower than any of them had ever been up against. If they failed, they knew they would meet a quick and merciless end.

As they sat on their horses waiting to leave, Parrott sought ways to calm their nerves. He stood in his stirrups, trying to speak over the nervous shuffling of the horses and men, but he soon realized that no one wanted to hear or even try to listen. Each man put his fear into his saddlebags in his own way; some took longer than others.

Parrott made one more attempt to calm his gang before they moved out. "Listen up. We'll call it off if things don't shape up by the time Cahn's bunch gets to the breaks by Joubert's Landing. I don't want to fight the army, either."

He looked around at his group. No more waiting. It was time to spring into action. "Did everybody bring a mask? I'm thinking they might string out a bit as they travel. If that happens, we can get each small bunch one by one. Let's go! We can't sit around here all day worrying about things."

Parrott spurred his horse hard, and it jumped forward and took off. This action provided the impetus for the reluctant gang, and they dutifully followed their leader.

The ride to the breaks was uneventful. The gang got well ahead of Cahn and the soldiers, positioning themselves at the bottom of a steep coulee near Joubert's Landing. Everyone donned their mask and Parrott rode back to the top to monitor the situation.

Before arriving at the coulee, Parrott's gang had traveled over an open, flat area that was several miles long. This part of the journey reinforced Parrott's notion that the Cahn group might string out and become divided because of laziness and overconfidence. After all, who was going to attack the army in broad daylight on flat, open ground?

Parrott was correct in his assessment. The Cahn group divided into small groups on the flat area with Cahn's wagon and a small group of soldiers in the lead. The steep coulee that Parrott had chosen was right at a turn in the trail, so the lead element would be out of sight of the others for a while.

* * *

THE GANG HAD BEEN WAITING for what seemed like an eternity, fidgety and nervous, when Parrott suddenly appeared at the bottom of the coulee. His eyes glowed, and a maniacal grin displayed dirty teeth. He said to the men, "OK, gents. This is it! When the first bunch gets to the turn at the top of the coulee, we'll jump them and take their guns away. Then we'll bring them down here and hold them until we waylay the next bunch. We'll grab the money and run when everybody is captured and disarmed. Time to get to work."

Parrott's plan worked to perfection. When the bandits appeared before Cahn and the first group of soldiers, the group was so stunned they put up no resistance. Nor did any of the other isolated groups. Before long, Parrott's small gang had captured fifteen soldiers and Cahn's wagon and money. Parrott's men loaded up the money, and the gang high-tailed it for Milestown, discarding their masks along the way.

The outlaw beamed with pride as he rode alongside Manuel Garcia. "Manuel, we just defeated the army! What do you think about that? Plus, we got rich. This might be the best day of my life!"

Manuel Garcia, who never smiled much, was grinning from ear to ear. "It is truly a miracle, Mr. Parrott. I never thought it would work."

"You're right, son. It is a miracle! We're gonna have some fun in town tonight! Ride hard, boys!"

It was the greatest job ever pulled off by George Parrott. He would eventually continue on in the world as a pair of shoes made from his skin, attending the Wyoming Governor's Inaugural Ball on the feet of the new governor.

* * *

MANUEL GARCIA, whose real name was Manuel Vaca and who would later become known as the Professor among his fellow ranch hands, grew up in the borderlands along the Rio Bravo in the Chihuahua region of Mexico.

He was raised in the tradition of and trained to be a vaquero. His family worked a small ranch and came by their notoriously wild cattle by purchase or raids across the river into Texas. It was a rugged and harsh country for both man and beast, demanding an equally tough and highly trained saddle horse. Manuel became a fine rawhide braider and gained the expertise and finesse to train fine, responsive horses that could work the country. He also gained a rudimentary education from the priests in the area and built upon that through focus and hard work, learning passable English along the way. But his personality was that of a wanderer; his thirst for adventure equaled his thirst for learning.

Vaca ended up in Montana because of happenstance. His family often raided across the river into Texas for cattle, as did families from the Texas side. Manuel looked forward to these raids, as they were the peak of excitement in his life, and he could test his skills against the Texans. Although the raids were dangerous, often resulting in a great deal of shooting and the occasional death, a certain camaraderie born of blood and sweat developed among the participants. There was an unwritten code of conduct among the adversaries, and life was not taken cheaply. This benefited everyone.

During one of these raids, contested by the Texans, they had taken the son of one of the wealthier Texas ranchers in the region hostage and had brought him back across the river. It wasn't a case of the boy being taken in a daring attempt; he had fallen off his horse and been picked up by Vaca's people before the Texans could rescue him. He represented quite a prize in terms of ransom. The men were excited at the prospect of the silver or cattle that could be exchanged for the boy.

In camp, the young Texan was lightly bound hand and foot, but not mistreated. He was terrified at first, but after being assured by Manuel that no harm would come to him, he settled down and the men freed his hands from the restraints. Manuel offered him food and a little mezcal, which the boy took eagerly. Soon, the young Texan became rather chatty. The alcohol had worked its magic and the two young men conversed. Before long, the talk turned to adventure and great things that could be had on the trail north.

Manuel listened intently as the Texan became animated, waving his hands as he spoke. "I'm tellin' you, Manuel. We should head north on one of the big drives. A cowpuncher on my daddy's place went on one and said the land was free and wild. No rules at all. A man could do almost anything with no law interfering. Lots of women in the saloons, booze, and fights with the natives. Danger everywhere. There's even buffalo still runnin' free up north as far as the eye can see. You can ride all day long and never run out of the wooly buggers."

Manuel carefully considered this information. This was the adventure he was seeking. "Are you sure of this?"

"Hell, yeah. I heard it straight from the horse's mouth. I'm fixin' to sign on with a drive soon and head out. Make my way in the world."

"How do you sign on with one of these drives? Are there good wages?"

The Texan thought for a moment, then said, "Well, you need to get up to Fort Worth first. Most of them leave out of there. They even give you a horse if you don't have one and tack it up, too. The bastards probably take it out of your wages, though. But I heard they pay good wages, so a man could probably cover it easy. Of course, guys like you and me are already outfitted, so we don't need anything. You should come with me, and we can partner up."

Manuel nodded in approval. It was settled. He would head to the north country and stake his claim. "I like your idea of seeing the north country. It's something different and, like you, I need to carve out my place in the world. I'm in with you, my friend."

* * *

JUST BEFORE THE Texan's release, Manuel and the young man came up with a time and meeting place from which they would start their journey to Fort Worth. Of course, neither family was informed of this plan. They just left and began their adventure, arriving in Fort Worth flat broke.

They had no trouble signing on with a drive. While they found adventure aplenty, they also found hard work, sleepless nights, fear, and death. Manuel lost his companion not long after they cleared the Texas border. It wasn't the result of a glamorous fight with the Comanche or a shootout with a desperado. No, it was gangrene. The Texan had suffered a deep cut on his leg, which he kept hidden and didn't properly clean. It wasn't long before infection set in, then gangrene, and by the time the young man failed to rise for his shift with the herd because of fever, it was too late. Buried where he died, they left him to rest forever in an unmarked grave on a lonely windswept plain.

Alone now, Manuel learned to keep a low profile. He kept speaking and interacting with others to a minimum, fitting in but not standing out. He was well-liked by the other cowboys because he was a skilled hand and highly knowledgeable about horses, even though he was only sixteen when he went up the trail in 1877. The cowboys did, however, like to tease him about what they saw as shyness. They didn't realize that in moments of silence, Manuel was constantly observing and learning to gauge situations. It kept him out of trouble more than once in his travels.

He also had the characteristic of being very light-skinned. Manuel's family was predominantly Spanish, with a bit of indigenous blood thrown in for good measure. He could pass for a gringo when needed, and this, along with his mannerisms, made him somewhat invisible among the raucous crowd found along the trail.

* * *

THE TRAIL ENDED IN MILESTOWN, Montana Territory. Relieved of his responsibilities and with no other plans, Manuel walked into the nearest saloon. Once at the bar, he ordered a shot of whiskey and glanced at the man next to him, who had a large nose that dominated his face. The man looked back at Manuel, taking him in from head to toe. He smiled and said, "My name is George. You look like a cowboy in need of a job."

Manuel nodded. "Yes, you're right. I just finished a drive, and I need work."

"You're in the right place, son. I've got a spot for you. Are you particular about your work? I need a man who can work hard and keep his mouth shut. Can you do that?"

Manuel didn't see these as particularly onerous requirements and he said, "Yes, sir. I don't talk much, and I work hard. I can do your work."

"How are you with horses?"

"I was raised to be a vaquero, sir. I know horses like the back of my hand."

"That's what I suspected. It looks like you got yourself a job." George Parrott reached over and shook Manuel's hand, then patted him on the back. "You're drinking on me tonight. I'll take you back with me when we're done here. You can meet the men and we'll get you a spot to bed down."

Parrott took a drink of whiskey and continued, "We got a few horses outside of town here. We'll move them to the center of the territory, hole up for a spell, and then sell them up in Canada."

Motioning to the bartender, the outlaw said, "Hey, barkeep! This young feller is drinking on me tonight. Make sure you take care of him. For that matter, buy the whole stinking saloon a drink. I'm feeling generous tonight."

Parrott grinned at Manuel. "Glad to have you on board, son. Have fun tonight. The hard part starts tomorrow. Do you have a gun?"

"Yes, I have a fine pistol."

"Alright. Make sure you keep it in good order. It may save your life."

It started that simply. Manuel asked no questions and did as he was told, adopting the name Manuel Garcia. No one questioned it. In return, George Parrott treated him generously and as a full-grown man. He never talked down to Manuel and often consulted him about horses.

The gang's primary way of making money was holding stolen horses in the Upper Musselshell area until they could sell them in Canada. The Canadians wanted horseflesh and didn't care about its origin. After they were flush with money from selling the stolen horses, Parrott and his gang always gravitated to Milestown, where Parrott spent lavishly until his money was gone. Then the cycle would repeat, with some of the criminal activity involving jobs other than stolen horses.

Parrott's downfall eventually arrived as a hanging in Wyoming because of the killing of a sheriff's deputy and railroad detective after a botched train robbery. This led to the outlaw becoming a pair of shoes, a fate Parrott would have found humorous. Manuel had refused to go on that ill-fated trip, and always said a little thanks to the man above that he had declined.

For his part, Manuel saved much of his money, keeping it in a hidden spot in the Upper Musselshell that only he knew, and with his share from the Cahn robbery, had a little cabin built in the foothills of the Castle Mountains. After the demise of Parrott, Manuel stayed in the area and, over the years, worked on various ranches to make ends meet, only dipping into his stash when absolutely necessary or to buy books. The cabin was his sanctuary when he needed time away from the ranches and people.

Manuel Vaca stayed mostly on the legal side of the trail in the period after riding with Parrott. Every once in a while, a few sheep or cows went missing, but nothing could be traced to him. Loss of livestock occurred all the time, and the cause wasn't always clear. As was his way, he maintained a low profile, continuing to keep the last name Garcia, and he enjoyed being called the Professor by the ranch hands. He believed no one knew he was the Garcia who had once ridden with Parrott long ago. How could they? Vaca had never made a spectacle of himself, and most people no longer remembered Parrott, or his gang.

But now he was feeling his years. The aches in his body told him that his time as a ranch hand was coming to an end. Something needed to be done. The desire to return to the borderlands, to his people, was occupying his thoughts more and more.

* * *

WHISTLING CONTENTEDLY, Vaca rode into Martinsdale atop a fine palomino. He was always well mounted; it was a matter of pride and prudence. Who could predict what would happen on any day? It was best to be on a good horse.

The seed of an idea in his mind had now germinated into a full-blown course of action. He was going to rob a bank! No, not on this day, but soon. Today, he was going to make a preliminary inspection of the bank. Sort things out so that he would have the best chance of success on the day of the heist. The plan would come together piece by piece as he made his inspection.

Manuel's eyes narrowed as he scanned the main street for the quiet State Bank of Martinsdale. He pulled his horse to a stop in front of the bank and stared at the building. It was small, secluded, and packed with cash. Perfect for a one-man job. A one-man job was not the best of circumstances, to be sure, but forming a gang at this point was out of the question.

He closed his eyes and envisioned himself fleeing out of town, bag full of stolen money in hand, galloping away toward the mountain peaks he knew so well. All it would take was one successful visit to pull it off.

* * *

MANUEL HAD QUIT his employment with the J-Bar-T soon after Colt's departure, retiring to his cabin to read a little and map out his future. As he tethered his horse outside the bank, he grinned. It felt good to be sure of one's actions, even though those actions ran askew of the law. It wouldn't be long, and he would be on his way back to the borderlands. Hopefully flush with enough money to live comfortably for the rest of his life.

The State Bank of Martinsdale was housed in a small, gable-front building with a sloping shed in the back. It was not a substantial building, being made of wood, and it sat next to a small saddlery business. The building would not have inspired confidence in a new bank customer, but that was not the issue. Manuel knew that a would-be robber must be quiet and quick. The town was small, and the buildings were close together. Any trouble in the bank would bring an immediate response from the townspeople. Greed would be deadly. The key to success would rest on getting what money he could quickly grab. Then, calmly leave and go hell-for-leather until a safe distance could be achieved.

Manuel entered the bank slowly, his eyes taking in the layout discreetly. The clerk looked up from his work and greeted him.

"Good day, sir. How can I be of help?"

Manuel walked up to the bank counter and said, "I would like to open an account here. I work on the ranches in the area, and I need a safe place to store my wages. I only have ten dollars in coins. Can I open an account with this amount? I am not a rich man."

The clerk smiled and nodded his assent. "You most certainly can. Being wealthy is not a requirement to hold an account here. Ten dollars is perfectly fine. Let me get my ledger, and we'll get started."

While the clerk retrieved his ledger from a desk, Manuel made note of the interior. The bank counter was substantial and caged, with a small opening to pass things back and forth. Only one person was working, but that person would have to be sufficiently scared to be brought to heel and turn over any loot. If any customers were in the bank at the time of the robbery, they would also have to be cowed. That would be easy enough. The threat of death usually did the trick for most people. Plus, customers might be an additional source of money.

The lock on the bank vault was unknown. It was most likely a timed lock, and that would make the vault unavailable if it was locked on the big day. Too much time would be wasted in getting it open. Was there a cash drawer or a small vault under the counter? He would find out shortly.

The clerk returned to the counter, opened his ledger, and prepared to write. "OK, sir. Let's get started. What did you say your name was?"

"My name is Garcia. Manuel Garcia."

"That's easy enough. Let me write your name in the ledger, along with a ten-dollar deposit."

The clerk wrote quickly, then looked at Manuel. "Can I have the ten dollars, please?"

Manuel retrieved silver dollars from his pocket and pushed the coins through the opening in the cage. "Here are the ten dollars and a little more. I didn't realize I had the extra coins. Must be getting forgetful in my later years. I would like to turn the additional coins into paper money, if that is possible."

"We can certainly do that, Mr. Garcia."

The clerk counted out the silver dollars, reached into his pocket to retrieve a key, and then stooped down to unlock something under the counter. Manuel closely noted this action. So, there was a cash box or a small safe under the counter. How much did it hold? If the main vault wasn't available on the day of the heist, it would have to suffice.

The clerk soon stood back up, passed the paper money to Manuel, then raised a hand.

"I almost forgot to give you a receipt for your deposit. Excuse my carelessness."

The clerk hurriedly filled out a receipt and passed it to Manuel.

"Does this conclude our business for to-day, Mr. Garcia?"

"Yes, sir. It does."

"Thank you for banking with us, and we look forward to seeing you in the future. Have a good day."

With a humorous glint in his eyes, Manuel said, "Thank you, too. I will visit again soon. Good day."

He casually left the bank, slowly approached his horse, and stood beside it, thinking.

I can do this job. There is a cash drawer or a small vault of some sort. It has coins and paper money. I'll only go for that if it comes down to it. The vault is surely on a timed lock. It may be out of the question. I can quickly deal with one clerk and any customers. I will be in and out before anybody knows what's happening.

Why not try for the vault? I guess I'll try to get the clerk to open it, but I'm not going to mess with it for long. Time won't be on my side. But the clerk will either open the cash drawer or whatever it is and give me the contents or be shot. A flour sack should work to hold the money. There is no need to bother with a mask. They'll never see me around here again.

Garcia is such a common name; no one will be able to trace me. After I leave the territory, I will call myself by my real name, and none of them know that name. I don't stand out in how I look. My description won't be a problem. This is going to work out well. If I can get money from the main vault, it will work out very well.

Satisfied with what he had seen in the bank, Manuel untied his horse from the hitching post, climbed into the saddle, and rode out of town toward his cabin.

HOMECOMING PARTY

*J*im Evinrude had gathered all the ranch hands and other employees of the J-Bar-T in front of the main ranch house the day before he went to Harlowton to pick up Janel and the relatives. The house was a majestic Victorian home, originally constructed to please his wife. It was spacious, with an elegant turret, stained glass, and elaborate woodwork throughout the building. It stood in stark contrast to the other construction on the ranch, which consisted of the utilitarian outbuildings and corrals found on any large spread in the area.

Since the death of Evinrude's wife due to what a doctor believed to be pneumonia, a bit of the shine had come off the building, but it was still in good condition. The death of her mother was the reason that Janel had left the ranch. There were too many memories that conjured up sadness, and she wanted a fresh start in a new place and a drastically different setting. She had found it among her relatives in New York City.

There was much speculation and talking among those gathered about the subject the J-Bar-T owner would discuss, and everyone was waiting for the boss to make his appearance. It didn't take long. Evinrude appeared, seemingly out of nowhere, and walked up onto the porch of the house. He looked around for a moment, then raised his hands for silence.

"Now listen up, everyone. Quiet! Listen up. As you all know, Janel is coming back for a brief visit from the east. We're going to throw a big ole party in her honor. She's also got some East Coast relatives traveling with her. My wife's sister and her son, New York City, born and bred. I have no idea what these people expect to see out here in Montana."

A murmur rippled lightly through the

crowd. Evinrude again raised his hands for silence.

"Alright, alright. Keep it down. I'm thinking they expect to see a full-on Wild West show of some type. Therefore, I propose we throw a good old-fashioned free-for-all barn dance. Of course, we'll invite all the best people from around the area, if we can find any. What does everyone think?"

One old ranch hand stepped forward. "Ain't those people from the big city kinda stuffy? Maybe we need to throw a real proper party. You know, with fancy vittles and music. An old-fashioned barn dance might be too much for their delicate minds to handle."

Evinrude and the crowd laughed. "You might be right. Those Easterners are likely to be pretty sensitive to our ways. Plenty of alcohol might loosen them up a bit. I can say without a doubt that my wife's sister, Mary, is as stuffed up an East Coaster as a person can find. Even alcohol may not cure what ails her. Anyway, let's get to discussing things. Time's a wasting."

A spirited debate ensued. Some believed the visitors would be put off if a traditional barn dance took place, and they advocated for a proper dinner party. Others just as vigorously took Evinrude's position that the guests would expect to see a Wild West shindig. Evinrude let the debate go on for some time, amused at the seriousness with which the participants put forth their opinions.

But the time for a decision was at hand, and the J-Bar-T boss had listened to enough debate. He waved the proceedings to a halt and said, "OK! It's time for a vote and a decision. We'll decide on it by a show of hands. None of you shady characters better raise more than one hand. This is going to be a fair and square vote."

Anticipation hung heavily in the air, and Evinrude paused for effect before saying, "Everybody in favor of a fancy, East Coast dinner and stuffy music, raise your hands."

A couple of hands went up in the air.

"Well, that's disappointing. I didn't think that anyone would vote for a stuffy party. Now, everybody in favor of a free-for-all, Wild West barn dance, raise your hands."

A cheer went up from the assembled ranch residents, and many thrust their hands in the air.

Evinrude grinned like a Cheshire cat. "That's more like it. A wild barn dance it is! Let's get moving on sorting things out. We need to get food, booze, and invitations delivered. Gussy the place up a bit. Plus, we still have a ranch to run. Let's get to work, everybody!"

Preparations for the dance in the large livestock barn earnestly began.

* * *

EVINRUDE PLANNED the dance for a Saturday. When the big day finally arrived, the J-Bar-T was buzzing with excitement. Even Mary was more animated and cheerful than usual, although she did her best to hide it, not wanting to provide Jim with too much satisfaction.

The guests began arriving at the J-Bar-T around dusk. Janel, her father, and Mary and Dalton made up the greeting committee. Mary was dressed in the formal, dignified manner of a New York socialite, as was Dalton, who wore a tuxedo tailored by one of the finest clothing stores in that city. Jim Evinrude dressed in the simple costume of a cowboy, in keeping with his belief that the height of fashion was a bath, a shave, and clean clothes.

Janel had gone back and forth throughout the day on her choice of dress, consulting Mary. She had brought both the latest fashions and simple country clothing.

"Aunt Mary, I can't decide on what to wear. I know many of the people who'll be at this party, and I don't want to offend them by not dressing in their manner. I think I should adopt simple country dress."

This argument did not sway Mary. "A young lady should dress in her finest. You have access to the best fashions now. There is no reason to be a country bumpkin. You should be a shining example to the young ladies attending. Give them something to aspire to. I'm going to wear my finest."

Janel rolled her eyes and said, "I would expect you to, and they will too. After all, you are from the big city. But I was once a simple country girl from around here. The girls will see me as uppity if I try to outdress them. I've decided. I'm going with something simple."

And so, Janel stood with the greeting party in a cotton gingham dress with a red floral plaid pattern and a wide collar. Lace-up trail boots, a wide-brimmed hat, and a red hair tie completed her outfit. It surprised her when the local girls began showing up in the latest East Coast fashions, likely obtained in Helena or Billings.

The best dressed of all was an old friend, Kaari Haugen. Janel looked Kaari over from head to toe and smiled. She lightly hugged her friend and said, "Goodness, Kaari! You certainly are a vision. Your fashion sense is impeccable." Mary tilted her head in Janel's direction and gave her a smug look. Janel shrugged her shoulders and chuckled.

Dalton's appearance created quite a stir. While the young ladies thought him a dashing, handsome young gentleman, the cowboys in attendance looked at him in bewilderment. There were more than a few snickers and raised eyebrows. They had come in their cowboy finest. Fancy spurs, colored shirts, and bright neckerchiefs were the order of the day.

The addition of the two Easterners to the country crowd created a certain amount of awkwardness among the people. Although mingling and polite conversation were taking place, the party was slow to get going. Jim Evinrude didn't like what he was seeing. This was supposed to be a party, and something needed to be done to make things more festive.

Jim called some of his men over to him. "Alright, boys. I'm having no more of this polite chit-chat. Break out the whiskey and the chokecherry wine. Get some music going and fire this dance up."

Soon, music from the fiddler's bow twanged and sang, and notes licked and teased the air. Cups of amber whiskey and chokecherry wine were poured, and in no time at all, the liquids worked their magic. Jim watched as one by one, folks began to move in an easy jig step around the barn floor, laughter ringing out like chimes. Dalton and Mary talked quietly to one side, away from the others, their manner rigid and unsure.

Jim shook his head; it was time for the relatives to loosen up. He walked over with two cups brimming with liquid cheer and held them out. "Dalton, you drink this one here and, Mary, why don't you take a sip on this," he said, waving the other cup toward her.

Mary took the cup and wrinkled her nose. "What is this?"

"It's chokecherry wine, Mary. A very fine vintage, indeed. Made right here on the ranch."

Mary sniffed at the cup. "It does smell good. I suppose a little couldn't hurt."

She took a sip, then a bigger drink. "This is quite good. I may have to have some more."

Jim laughed. "There's plenty of it."

Turning to Dalton, he quickly leaned back. "Sonofagun, Dalton. You drank that whiskey right down!"

Dalton nodded sheepishly. "Yes, sir. I didn't mean to drink it so fast. It is excellent whiskey. Can I have some more?"

Mary scowled at Dalton, and she spoke sharply to him, her words spilling out in a staccato tempo. "What do you know of whiskey? Have you been up to things I don't know about?"

Dalton looked around, like a child who had just been caught stealing cookies. "Nope. Friends have told me that whiskey's good, that's all. I was just being polite by saying how good it is."

Jim smiled knowingly. "Let the young

man have some fun, Mary. It's not every day a New Yorker finds himself at an honest-to-goodness barn dance. Alright, you two, get over there and get some more liquid refreshment. It'll do you both some good. You never know, if you drink enough, you might even find yourselves doing a little dancing."

Dalton watched as a change washed over his mother with every sip of wine. Her eyes sparkled, her cheeks pinked, and she chatted freely with everyone around her. After a third cup, Jim encouraged her onto the dance floor. She went willingly, and with every beat of the music, her movements grew more fluid. She swayed with abandon to the sound of the fiddle, throwing her head back in laughter.

Jim clapped his hands and chuckled, amused at Mary's transformation. He turned to a man next to him and said, "I can't believe it. Mary is having a dancing fit. It's amazing what a little chokecherry wine can do for a person."

The same transformation also occurred with Dalton. The whiskey had taken him from sullen and awkward to being a friendly and charming companion. As he walked off the dance floor with a pretty young woman on his arm, he extolled the free life and told his partner of his plans to live in a wild country like Montana, facing and overcoming danger. Seeking and finding romance. She giggled in approval.

* * *

ANOTHER CUP of whiskey burned Dalton's throat and came to rest far away, in the back of his brain. A sudden thought broke free and floated lightly through his mind. He felt elation as he hurried over to Evinrude.

"Mr. Evinrude, I would like to do a song for the crowd! Vaudeville style. I believe I possess the ability to do a good job."

Evinrude raised an eyebrow. "Um ... OK, son. Are you sure you want to do that? This is a pretty tough crowd. Do you have any experience?"

"Yep. I've done some performing in my school days. I'm up to the task."

"Well, alright. I'll announce you, and you can have at it."

Evinrude stepped forward and silenced the music and crowd. A hush fell over those assembled. He took off his hat and held it to his heart. Lifting his chin in the air, he said, "Ladies and gentlemen. Straight from New York City, I present to you, Dalton. He will now perform a song for you fine people. Give him a little room, please."

Dalton strode to the center of the barn with confidence in his stride and pride in his chest. He stood up straight and held out one arm in a grandiose fashion, as though he were reaching for something just beyond his grasp. He loudly said, "I will perform the great American classic 'I Met My Gal in Frisco.'"

Whispers and isolated laughter percolated through the crowd. People looked at each other with confused expressions. No one had ever heard of this song.

Dalton cleared his throat, and his feet began to move in an awkward march. His arms swung exaggeratedly, and he launched into the song. A few in the crowd laughed at first, then their laughter was erased by claps that followed Dalton's rhythm. His voice rose in volume and intensity with each word, his marching steps proudly pounding on the floor like drums. The crowd's claps became ever livelier, interspersed with hoots and hollers. After singing the last word, Dalton bowed dramatically, sending waves of applause throughout the building.

Janel giggled and clapped with glee. She clapped even louder and said, "Dalton is drunk as hell, but he sure did a good job!"

After Dalton's rousing performance, the drinking and merriment began anew. The Easterners, who had once been outsiders, were now firmly embraced as part of the crowd. Ranch hands brought food in and laid it out to help temper the effects of the alcohol; the partygoers eagerly enjoyed the feast.

AMONG THE RENEWED PARTYING, Jim Evinrude was talking to a fellow rancher when he noticed a familiar face at the entrance to the barn. He excused himself and walked up to the new guest, offering his hand. The cowboy gripped it firmly, and the two men shook hands.

"Colt! How the hell are you doing, son? I'm glad you could make it. How are your new endeavors going? You ready to come back to the ranch yet?"

"No, sir. I'm stickin' to my new occupation. I've been doing pretty well so far, Mr. Evinrude."

"That's great to hear, Colt. Come on in and enjoy yourself."

Evinrude pointed to Janel. "If you look right over there, you'll see a pretty blonde girl. That's my daughter, Janel. Why don't you go over and introduce yourself, but don't get any foolish ideas, you hear?"

Colt grinned. "No, sir. I won't."

Evinrude then pointed out Mary and Dalton.

"Now, over there … See that young man in the fancy suit and the older woman in the equally fancy dress? Those are relatives of mine. Make sure you say hello to them, too."

Colt nodded and took off directly for Janel, who was talking to a group of young women. He would introduce himself to the relatives later. For now, there was only one thing on his mind, and he quickened his step as he got closer to the object of his desire.

Noticing some motion, Janel looked away from the woman she was talking to and saw a tall cowboy staring at her as he approached. Green eyes! She recognized him in an instant. Her breathing increased, her pupils became bright, dark saucers, and she blushed. What would possess the train robber to show up here? She could not speak, a rare condition for her.

Janel's reaction amused Colt. He stopped directly in front of her, his eyes roaming over her and lingering here and there. He was close, uncomfortably close, and it caused Janel to blush even more.

Colt addressed her with confidence. "Good evening, Miss Evinrude. Your father said to come on over here and say hello. I used to work on this spread before I went on to other things."

Janel regained the power of speech, but barely. She opened her mouth and a tentative squeak emerged. She cleared her throat and tried again, this time managing to croak out a weak "Hello." In a high-pitched voice, she said, "How did you get here?"

Colt chuckled. "By horseback, ma'am. Same as a lot of folks here, I suspect. That seems like the transportation of choice in these parts."

Janel was embarrassed by her question. She glanced around at the other women and saw that the cowboy equally entranced them.

This irritated her, and she frowned for a moment, then smiled brightly at Colt. She had fully regained her composure.

"I know how you got here, silly. I'm pleased to meet your acquaintance. What is your name?"

"My name is Colt Matson."

"You certainly are a bold character to walk into this group of ladies. But I guess boldness isn't a problem for you. What are your intentions, cowboy?"

"I'm searching for a dance partner, and you look like a gal who can dance."

Janel nodded in agreement. "You are right about that. Let's get to dancing."

She pulled Colt over to the dancing area of the barn. The musicians were playing a waltz, and the two began to dance. It quickly became apparent to Janel that Colt was a skilled dancer, and he didn't miss a beat as they moved around. She beamed in admiration, leaning a little closer to him. The golden-haired beauty equally impressed Colt. They seemed to be the only two people in the barn as they spun around to the music.

After a few dances and drinks, Janel was

ready for some fresh air. She moved in close to Colt, barely on the right side of propriety.

"What do you say we go out the back and get some fresh air? It's getting hot in here."

A smile flickered across Colt's face. "That sounds good to me."

They left the raucous scene in the barn and walked out the back to a cool, pleasant evening. There were several other couples out back chatting and laughing. Janel walked to a spot just out of earshot of the others and turned to face Colt.

Now her pleasant, flirty manner changed. She was tense, and a look of exasperation was on her face. "You must be either the bravest man I've known or just a plain old lunatic. I can't figure out which one it is. Why would you take such a chance? Coming here like this?"

Her firm tone delighted Colt, and he quickly said, "After I saw you on the train, I just had to see you again. I heard about this party and figured I'd still be welcome on the ranch. Besides, you're the only one here who knows what I've been up to. I wasn't sure you'd recognize me, but I could tell straight away that you did when I walked up to you in the barn. How could you recognize me so easy?"

"Your green eyes! Those bright green eyes. I'd recognize them anywhere. Plus, the fact I've lived around cowboys most of my life. I could quickly tell on the train you were a cowboy and not some seasoned desperado."

Colt shrugged. "Dang, I sure hope nobody else figured it out."

Janel softened, and she decided to lie. She had told the sheriff her theory, so at least one other person might have figured it out; others probably had too. And if the sheriff had latched on to her theory, that would be a mountain of trouble for Colt. But she didn't want to trouble him right now. The fact was, she liked him despite his train robbing ways.

"Don't worry. I don't think anybody else has figured out you're just a cowboy from around here, but you might want to change your look some. I mean, you stick out like a sore thumb with that look."

Janel's remark offended Colt, and he put his hands on his hips. "What do you mean, that look? I'm cowboy through and through, just like the old days. I'm the real deal."

She chuckled and twirled a strand of hair

between her fingers. "That might be true, and believe me, I like your look. But you're a pretty recognizable man in that garb. You need to work in the moving picture business. You'd make a splendid cowboy in films. A real crackerjack. Then you wouldn't have to worry about life behind bars, or worse."

"Don't worry about me, gal. I can handle my affairs well enough. Hey, do you want some more wine? I could use a little more firewater. I'll be right back."

Colt took off for the drinks before Janel could respond. She sighed and started to think.

He sure is handsome. What could a brief fling hurt for a few days? Could it be more than a fling? Maybe I can talk him into returning to New York and working with me at Biograph. All the folks there would love him. It might save his life. Right now, he can leave the area, and that would be the end of it. I wonder what other craziness he's got planned. Oh, he's coming back with the drinks. Don't let him know you like him too much.

Colt returned, a sly grin playing across his lips as he handed Janel her cup of wine. She smiled back at him reflexively, her blue eyes glittering in the moonlight. He felt electricity run through him, and it seemed as if time had stopped for a moment, and all that existed was their connection. Her blue eyes were bottomless pools he could have fallen into, never wanting to escape. Why was he so smitten with this girl? This had never happened before.

He said quietly, "Damn, girl, when you look at me like that, it's like the entire world just stops." Then he gently brushed a strand of hair away from her face.

She sighed softly and looked shyly away. "You're drunk, cowboy."

"A little, I guess, but I mean what I'm saying. I might be fixin' to steal a little kiss from you."

"What's stopping you?"

Colt leaned in and their lips met. Her body melted against his, as if she'd known him for years. Laughter and the faint trickle of music suddenly reminded Janel that others were around, and maybe they had gone too far. She pulled away from Colt, her cheeks flushed. What would people think? Especially her father if he found out. They both fidgeted awkwardly, a little embarrassed, but there was no regret. Silence prevailed for a few moments, both too afraid to break it.

Janel was the first to speak. "You need to get out of this place. Come to New York. Like I said, you'd be able to make it as an actor."

Colt flipped a hand up and said, "That moving picture business is strange to me. People paying money to see things that happen in real life. Besides, I'm a cowboy in real life. An adventurer too. I've just gotten started on adventurin'."

"That's what you call robbing trains?"

"Yes, ma'am. I've got big plans. Maybe when I'm done, I'll take you up on the moving picture business."

There was sadness in her voice as she said, "It'll come to a terrible end, Colt."

Colt moved some dirt with his foot. "It's possible, but if I get in a bad spot, I'll just think of your smile, and that'll make everything OK."

Janel leaned over, put her head on Colt's shoulder for a second, then pulled back.

"Colt, you can be anything you want in the moving pictures and go anywhere. My director, Mr. Griffith, is thinking about moving the entire operation to California. He thinks there will be more freedom there for the business. You'd love California, and there are real cowboys like you. You wouldn't have to stay in New York too long, and you'd be back West. Not Montana, but still someplace good."

"Hmm. I'll give it some thought, Janel. I really will. But I got to do some adventurin' first. Get it out of my system before I even think about it."

Before Janel said anything in return, a young woman walked outside the barn and yelled out in jest, "Hey, y'all! Mind your manners! No illegal stuff. Sheriff Sedgwick just showed up at the dance."

Horrified, Janel looked frantically toward the barn. She grabbed Colt by the arm and said, "Colt, you need to leave! You need to leave now!"

Colt didn't argue. Janel was right. It was time to go. "I want you to meet me at my camp. Here, lean over, and I'll whisper the way to it in your ear."

Janel didn't understand why Colt wanted to whisper the location. There was nobody close enough to hear their conversation. But she indulged Colt and leaned over. Colt divulged the location of his camp to her, adding that he would just be lying about for a few days, making plans. Janel told him she would come and visit him whenever she had a chance. Then he left her and was quickly out of sight. She sighed deeply and returned to the dance with a look of sadness, shuffling slowly toward the entrance to the barn.

When Janel entered the barn, her father walked up to her. Jim had noted that Colt and Janel had been spending a lot of time together at the dance. When he asked her where Colt had gone, she tried to look relaxed. "He had to go. Something about work he had to do early in the morning. He told me to tell you thanks for the festivities."

Jim hugged Janel and said, "Come with me and talk to the sheriff. He'll be happy to chat with you for a spell. It's always a good idea to keep the law happy."

* * *

JANEL WAS ALMOST at Colt's camp. Her mood swung back and forth between happiness and sadness. This would be their last meeting before she left for the east in a little over a week. She couldn't risk any more meetings, not for her sake or his; too many questions were being asked about where she went on her "rides," as she called them.

She would give it one more chance to convince him to change paths and come to New York and then on to California. But she was leaving; that was set in stone. Her future didn't lie in Montana anymore. She loved her work in the moving pictures, and she would not give it up for anyone. Why couldn't Colt see it was the future? It would give him all the adventure he sought without the terrible risk. She was falling for the foolish cowboy. That was true. But she wouldn't throw her future away on it. Colt had to come to his senses and change course, or they couldn't be together.

Janel left the game trail along the railroad tracks and rode down through the tall grass into Colt's camp. Colt was sitting against a tree reading one of his pulp magazines and immediately jumped to his feet when he saw her. He quickly stuffed the magazine into a saddlebag and walked over to greet her. She waved from the horse and rode over to him, smiling as best she could. When she stopped her horse, Colt helped her to the ground.

"Dang! You're looking as lovely as ever, Janel."

Janel blushed a little and said, "Why, thank you, dear sir. Please tie my horse to something, so he doesn't run off."

Colt bowed to her solemnly, like a butler. "Of course, ma'am."

She handed Colt the reins and watched as he secured the animal. Then, they both walked into the campsite and sat down.

Janel looked at Colt quizzically. "Colt, why did you pick this particular spot for a campsite? Many places would've worked just as well, maybe even better."

"I don't know. It was a pretty good place to work out of for the train robbery. And … It's kinda dumb. I don't want to say."

"Get it out, Colt. I want to hear it."

Colt chuckled and looked at the ground. "OK. Here it goes. When I was a child, I used to go down to the river with a girl to a spot just like this one. She was a neighbor girl, and we were friends. We'd go to the river and play around and stuff. Throw sticks in the water. Run through the trees.

"If the ground was muddy, we'd make mud pies or balls and throw them at each other. Sometimes we'd sit around and look at the mountains or the water. Maybe hold hands. The memories of those times kinda stick with me, I guess."

"Wow, Colt! You must've been in love with her."

"Love! We were just young folks. Ten or eleven, if I remember correctly. What can you know about love at that age?"

Janel tossed a twig at Colt. "I think you can know a lot about love at that age, even if you don't realize what it is. Love is a big thing and covers a lot. Like a big, warm blanket."

Colt picked up a twig and tossed it back at her. "Maybe. I ain't no expert on love."

He pondered love for a few moments, then said, "I suppose there's love that fills you up real quick and then spills over. And then there's another kind that you find in silence, just sitting quietly with someone you care about. Oh heck, what do I know about it?"

Janel smiled, thinking about what Colt had said. "You might know more than you think, Colt."

They spent the rest of the day in comfortable idleness. Sometimes sitting in silence, sometimes chatting. Colt even showed Janel his Western pulp magazines, and they both read from them for a while, talking about the stories. They acted out a few parts, falling to the ground and laughing after they were done.

But soon, the day passed. It was time for Janel to leave. She made one more attempt to convince Colt to come with her, but it was to no avail. Colt was dead set on continuing his adventuring, and his mind was not changing.

Janel retrieved her horse, and Colt helped her into the saddle. Both were silent for what seemed like forever, neither one wanting to say the inevitable goodbye until Janel reluctantly spoke.

"Colt, I know I can't change your mind. But you be careful. I hope you get done with this business soon and come out to see me. I'll be looking for you. It's been a grand time with you this short while, but I have to leave to go back east soon, and it's too risky to visit anymore."

Colt's body sagged; he understood the situation. "I know. But it has been special. Don't worry about me. I can take care of myself. I promise I will get out to you when I get this adventurin' out of my system. Then we can

EVERETT RIGGS

both be famous in the moving pictures. Of course, I won't be going by Cottonwood Kid then. That name might be a little too well-known. Say, I want to know if I can tell folks you're my gal."

Janel bit her lip to keep from crying, and her eyes moistened. She looked away from Colt and said, "Of course, you can tell people I'm your gal. I sure do hope we are together someday, Cottonwood Kid."

She started her horse and left, tears just beginning to gush from her eyes. Janel rushed out of sight, wanting to get away as quickly as possible. It felt like she was leaving a funeral.

A VISITOR

$\mathcal{C}$olt felt a strange mix of emotions after Janel left. Excitement and loneliness, ambition and disappointment, hope and sadness. He moped around the campsite, languidly fishing in the nearby river and flipping through his pulp magazines. In his mind, his adventuring so far had been a wild success. He was a known man, the Cottonwood Kid, with a romantic interest to boot. Why the bad feelings? Sure, it was unlikely their crossing of paths would amount to anything; Janel was leaving for the east. But that shouldn't trouble an adventurer. He still had things to do in this neck of the woods. Or did he? There was a bit of heat that was starting to tickle the back of his neck, and it didn't feel good. It was time to get back to planning and acting. Sitting around wouldn't accomplish anything. Maybe he would become a dashing cowboy in the moving pictures after he finished adventuring. That was somewhere down the trail. Colt still believed that he had a future ahead of him.

He had a vague idea to head south toward Big Timber. His thoughts drifted to Gordy Hale, a fellow cowboy he knew from the Cornwall Brothers Ranch who had gone out on his own and built himself a small spread in the Melville area. Colt was sure Gordy wouldn't mind him swinging in for a quick visit. He would only need a day, or two at most, to get his bearings straight and settle on new plans before moving on to greener pastures.

A kernel of truth now penetrated Colt's thick skull. He needed to quit the Harlowton area for good if he wanted to stay ahead of trouble. An adventurer like him needed to be a rolling stone. That settled it. He was heading for Gordy's place.

There might be something of interest to be found around Melville, too. Colt knew little about the community other than his father telling him that Norwegians had settled the area. He hadn't known what his father meant by that statement. He'd concluded that Norwegians must be people of nefarious character, but Colt had never met anyone from Norway. However, Gordy knew Melville well, and would know what to do. All options were open, and that made Colt smile.

Colt quickly broke camp and tacked up Buck. Sliding into the saddle, he pulled his hat low on his head and tapped the horse lightly with his spurs. The trusty animal responded immediately, and off they went, with Colt informing his steed of his latest plans. The best part was Buck always seemed to agree with him on their course of action, never trying to dissuade him. People, on the other hand, never seemed to think much of his ideas. What did they know? Someday soon, he'd be famous, and everyone would listen to him.

"Buck, let's take a run down to Gordy's outfit. Get things sorted out a bit. He's always good for a few laughs and a tug on the bottle. I think he's married up now. There might be some good cookin' to be had. We'll get a new plan for adventurin'. Maybe ole Gordy will want to join in the fun."

* * *

GORDY HALE WAS NAILING a worn board to a corral post when he saw a rider coming his way. He squinted his eyes and stared intently, trying to determine if the rider was a friend or foe.

Hale had a rodent-like quality about him, from the wild tufts of black hair that covered his forehead to the beady eyes that seemed to shift quickly, cunningly taking in the surroundings. Hale was always searching for the upper hand.

He had a slightly upturned nose that was sprinkled with freckles. His education was limited, but he had a sharp intellect that allowed him to find an edge, even in the most unlikely situations. Hale took advantage of people, no matter the cost. Under the influence of alcohol, he became happy and carefree, almost to the point of mania. However, this could change quickly if things didn't go his way, and he was prone to violence.

Although a skilled cowboy, Hale didn't possess the constitution or inclination necessary to make his small ranch a going concern. The small, dilapidated property spoke only of poverty. Gordy spent most of his energy on drinking, gambling, and scheming. Petty theft and the occasional sale of an animal whose provenance was usually dubious funded the drinking and gambling. Only Hale's wife, a young woman who grew up accustomed to being poor, kept Gordy with at least one foot on the right side of the law, now and then. Long enough to do the work necessary to keep the ranch from falling down around them.

As the rider drew closer, Hale recognized the man in the saddle as none other than his old partner, Colt Matson. He was a little perplexed. Colt had never visited him at his home before, and recently, they had mainly seen each other occasionally in the saloons in Harlowton. Hale's criminal instincts told him something was up. What did Colt want? It didn't matter. Gordy was looking forward to some companionship and fun. Something to break up the monotony and dreariness of life.

He called out to Colt, "Hey, stranger! I haven't seen you in a while. Whatcha doing down in this country?"

Colt trotted his horse up to Hale and quickly dismounted. The two men shook hands.

"I'm in the adventurin' business now and thought I'd drift down this way."

"Adventurin' business? What the hell is that?"

"I ride around looking for adventure and make a little money in the process."

"So, you're an outlaw."

Colt paused and pondered Gordy's statement. Was he really just an outlaw? "I'm not completely outlawed up. In adventurin', a guy can go either way, legal or otherwise. I go by the name Cottonwood Kid."

Gordy jumped back a couple of steps, like a jolt of electricity had struck him. "I'll be a dirty dog! You're the one that robbed the Milwaukee over by Barber! There are wanted posters up all over the place. The law is after you, my friend. I reckon there're some steel bars in your future. You're just lucky the drawing they put on the poster doesn't look a damn thing like you. It's terrible."

Colt shrugged. "I was hoping I could lie up here for a day or two until I get straightened out on what I want to do."

Gordy looked sideways at his friend and said, "I don't know, Colt. You're a little hot to be staying around here." Then he spat on the ground and relaxed. "But ... I've never turned a friend down. You can stay in the barn for a couple of days if you need to. The wife doesn't know you're outlawing, so say nothing to tip her off."

Colt looked over at the drafty old barn. The smell didn't impress him.

"If it's all the same, I might just sleep outside."

"Suit yourself. Hey, something just popped into my head. Put your horse up and come into the house. We'll talk inside."

Hale went inside the house and sat down in a chair. He yelled out to his wife, "Delilah! An old friend just showed up. Will you bring me that bottle of whiskey in the kitchen? Get the kids out of the house. I have some business to discuss."

Delilah brought Hale the whiskey without

question. She had learned how to handle her husband's forceful behavior. She was rarely one to voice her opinion, which was usually the opposite of her spouse, who talked a lot and seemed to know everything. However, when Delilah did say something, Hale always paid attention. She had an inner strength that wasn't easy to spot under her slim figure.

Nothing about her face was particularly outstanding. It had a long shape and a nose that suited it. Her thick brown hair hung down on her shoulders, and there was a constant grimace on her face, almost like she was expecting bad news at any moment. Her big eyes gave the hint of having seen too much for her age. Oddly, Delilah never protested her husband's scheming, though it caused her to worry. If Gordy brought home money or goods, she didn't bother to ask how he came about them. It was enough if he provided, even though it was mostly meager. She could only keep him on the straight and narrow for brief periods of time.

She was curious about Gordy's friend, so she decided to lie low and play the situation by ear. Usually, the appearance of a friend meant trouble was soon to follow, but sometimes it meant money, and money was always in short supply around their home. She needed to get a handle on what was going to happen this time, and with this friend.

* * *

COLT KNOCKED on the door to the house, entered, and removed his hat. Gordy waved him in and pointed to a chair.

"Have a seat, Colt. I got a little liquid refreshment for us."

Hale took a drink from the bottle and passed it over to Colt, who did the same.

Hale rubbed his whiskers. "I've been doing some thinking lately on a little job that might pay. Now that I know you're in the adventurin' business, as you call it, I thought you might be interested in partnering up on it. It'll be a helluva lot of fun and pretty easy money, too."

Colt took another drink of whiskey and then passed the bottle to Hale.

"Whatcha got in mind? I've got no place to be."

"Over in Melville, they run a mail wagon down to Big Timber. As far as I can tell, it's just one man driving it. No guards. Can you believe that?"

"Ain't there a bunch of Norwegians over in Melville? My pa told me so."

Gordy shrugged, annoyed at Colt's question. "Yeah … So? A lot of Norwegians do live over there. They're nice enough. Kinda hard-headed. I hit one in the head with a big stick once in a scrap and all it did was stun him. Would've killed a normal man. They eat that strange fish. Call it lute … or something or other. It's treated with lye. I can't remember the name."

Colt raised an eyebrow. "That's hard to believe. Eatin' lye can't be good for a person. Why don't they catch some fish right out of the creek and fry'em up in a pan when they're still fresh? That's a good way to eat fish."

"How the heck do I know? I'm not a Norwegian. They must be from a rough place to like that lye fish. I guess they never caught on to catching fish out of the creek and frying them up in a little butter. Who's to say what's best? People eat all kinds of strange things."

Hale took a long drink out of the bottle and set it on the floor.

"Anyway, they sure don't guard their mail wagon, and that's what's important to us. In fact, I think the fool driver heads out tomorrow for Big Timber. I've been tracking the movements, looking for the right time to knock it off. And by golly, I think I just stumbled into the right time."

Colt ran his fingers through his hair and thought about the proposition.

"I don't see the profit in this venture. What are we going to do with letters and such? Can you sell those things?"

"No. I ain't never heard of selling letters. The post office collects money for mailing letters and other business. There's no bank in Melville and no stage to carry the mail or money down to Big Timber. Just this character who drives a wagon down there. Besides, people put money in their letters. Maybe there's some money to be had there, but there must be a pretty good haul in the money from mail business."

Colt leaned back in his chair. "Hmm. That sounds interesting to me. It'll probably be pretty easy. There's two of us and only one of him. He'll be armed, though. I'm a man who doesn't care much for being shot."

Hale put his head in his hands, exasperated, then looked up at Colt. "So? You're afraid of being shot now? For crying out loud, Colt, you just robbed a train! Now you're afraid of a half-wit wagon driver?"

Gordy pointed at Colt. "Look, the driver has to cross a bridge to get across the Sweet Grass River. We'll put one of us on each side of the bridge in the trees and waylay him from front and back. He won't even know what hit him. Then we'll tie him up. He'll sit there a long time before anyone comes along. We'll be long gone with the loot and headin' straight back here. I'm telling you, it's going to be a piece of cake job."

Colt was convinced. This was exactly the kind of adventure he was seeking. "Gordy, I'll throw in with you. This sounds like something that suits me. There should be good money in it, too."

Hale grinned. "That's good to hear, partner. We'll leave out of here around dark and get to the Sweet Grass sometime late tonight. We don't want any folks seeing us. I calculate he'll cross the river sometime in the late morning, and we'll be there waiting for him."

Leaning sideways, Hale looked toward the kitchen and rubbed his belly. "I'll get Delilah to cook us up a good supper before we head out. We can't be robbing anybody without a good meal in us."

Colt snorted as thoughts of the buffet on the train flickered through his mind. "That's a true statement. Good grub is always necessary when adventurin'."

Delilah had been listening in on the conversation. She was worried but knew there was no way to change Gordy's mind when he smelled easy money. Her worry concerned the risk of the job the men were talking about, but that worry also extended to what would happen if the men pulled the job off and Gordy had money in his pocket. She knew he might head for the saloons in Melville, which meant drinking and gambling. They were flat broke now, and if he ended up in jail or dead, that would be their end. She wrung her hands and went to prepare a meal.

MAIL WAGON
ADVENTURES

*O*nce the sun set, Colt and Gordy left
Gordy's ramshackle ranch and
spurred their horses into a gallop. They rode
hard toward the Sweet Grass River, which
was little more than a large creek. The bright
moonlight provided them with enough illu-
mination to guide their journey around
Melville. When they arrived at the river, they
wrapped the reins of their horses around a
gnarled tree, untacked them, and then tethered them with hobbles. The intrepid outlaws
hastily made camp upriver from the bridge
on the Melville side. Without bothering to
build a fire, they drank the last of their
whiskey before settling in for the night. All of

nature seemed to succumb to sleepiness at once and aided by the alcohol they had consumed throughout the day, Colt and Gordy quickly followed suit, each falling into a deep, peaceful sleep.

They woke to tiny rays of light filtering through the trees. Colt rubbed his eyes until they focused, then stretched his arms and yawned. He rolled over and looked at Gordy, who was stirring, fighting the urge to leave such a restful sleep.

"Gordy, what time did you say the mail wagon will come along?"

Hale rolled onto his back and looked at Colt. "Huh?"

"When is the mail wagon coming?"

"Relax, partner. It'll probably be here late morning or so. He doesn't move too fast in that wagon. You got anything to eat? I packed nothing. Figured we'd grab a steak in Melville when this is over."

"I don't know if going into Melville is that good of an idea after we rob this fella."

"Don't worry. Like I said yesterday, we'll have plenty of time before they find him. Now, darn it, do you have anything to eat? A guy gets pretty hungry in the morning."

"All I have is a little hardtack in the saddlebags. We can soak it in some water. I like to soak it in coffee, but I ran out of coffee."

"That's no good, Colt. I could use a cup of coffee. Hardtack and water will have to do."

Colt went to the river and filled a tin cup with water. The men divided the last of Colt's hardtack and took turns soaking it in the cup. They contentedly sat and ate the meager meal, enjoying the light breeze blowing through the trees. The breeze brought the hay-like smell of the sweet grass, causing Colt to grow sleepy again.

Suddenly, Hale said, "Colt, I was thinking. You have a name now, Cottonwood Kid. I need to have an outlaw name for this job. It ain't fair that you have one and I don't."

"What name do you want, Gordy?"

"I think I want to be called the Preacher."

Colt laughed, amused at the absurdity of Gordy's choice of name. "Preacher? I've never known you to do any ministering."

Hale, offended by Colt's laugh, scrunched his face and said, "An outlaw can have any name he wants! How do you know I can't do any preaching? I tell you, I've preached up a storm now and then—rained fire and brimstone down on folks. Real come to the Lord kind of stuff. Yep, that's my outlaw name. The Preacher."

Colt stretched his arms again. "Alright, if you say so. Maybe we should start getting prepared. We need to do something, or I might go back to sleep. It's so peaceful here, and the sweet grass smells good. It makes you drowsy."

Hale got up, went over to his saddlebags, and retrieved two old cloth sacks. He tossed one over to Colt, who stood up and examined the sack, turning it over in his hands as though he would discover some secret in the fabric.

Gordy pointed to his head. "We're going to put these on our heads. I didn't cut the eyes and mouth out on either one. I didn't want Delilah thinkin' we were up to no good. Do you have a knife to cut these sacks?"

Colt reached into his pocket and pulled out a small pocketknife. "Yeah. I got a little knife right here. It'll work, but it won't look too good. I guess it's not a beauty contest."

The two men cut out the sacks, placed them over their heads, and put their hats on, pulling them down tight. They looked at each other, suppressing the urge to laugh.

Hale couldn't help himself and burst out laughing. "My goodness. We look frightful indeed. This will scare the hell out of that mail driver. Let's go over our plan."

He quit laughing and paused, working out the details of the plan in his mind. "You'll ride down a bit and stay on this side of the bridge. Go below the bridge far enough to stay out of sight, but not too far. You need to be able to get to that driver quickly. I'll cross the bridge and go up the river a little. When he crosses over the bridge, I'll come out and confront him. That'll keep him lookin' at me. You ride in behind and get the drop on him from your direction. The bastard won't even know you're coming. How's that sound for a plan?"

Colt nodded in agreement. "Yep, that ought to work just fine. Do you have anything to tie this fellow up with?"

"Yeah. I brought some rope with me. If that doesn't work, we'll use your leather lariat."

Colt didn't care for that idea. He kicked at the ground, then put his hands on his hips. "I don't like that plan, Gordy. I'm kinda fond of

that lariat. Let's make sure the rope works."
Then, he clapped his hands loudly and said,
"OK! Let's get our horses rounded up and get
moving. A man needs to be on time."

The men retrieved their horses, saddled
up, and Colt set off below the bridge while
Hale crossed over it and disappeared out of
sight.

* * *

COLT CAREFULLY CHOSE HIS SPOT: a patch of
thick trees a good fifty yards below the
bridge. He rode into the trees, his horse
moving steadily as he gripped the reins
lightly, gently guiding the animal to a suitable
place to stop. Colt lazily dismounted from
the horse and sat down against a tree,
holding the reins loosely in one hand so the
horse could lower its head and nibble on the
rich grass. Slowly, his head drooped to his
chest as the morning warmth wrapped
around him like a cocoon. Colt's breathing
turned to soft snores, and he failed to notice
the mail wagon that was making its way to
the bridge. The horses clopped along quietly,
the wooden planks of the bridge creaking

softly as the weight of the wagon came onto it.

Suddenly, Colt felt the reins sharply tug in his hand as his horse abruptly raised its head, shaking him out of his sleep. Through half-open eyes, he glimpsed movement across the bridge. Not sure what was happening yet, he slowly got to his feet to get a better look and realized with a start that it was the mail wagon. On the other side of the bridge, Hale had been waiting patiently, fully alert.

Once the mail wagon crossed the bridge, Hale emerged from the trees and galloped his horse toward it, his poorly cut-out mask creating the appearance of a macabre ghoul bearing down on the driver. The driver's eyes widened in terror at the sudden appearance of Hale, and he reached frantically for the double-barreled shotgun resting at his side. Retrieving it, the driver fired a shot, but it just barely missed Gordy.

Startled by the shotgun blast, Hale's horse slid to an abrupt stop and reared up, sending Gordy crashing to the ground. For a moment, everything was still as death. Then Gordy groaned and tried to sit up, only to collapse again, lying on the ground motionless. Meanwhile, his horse had taken off down a game path alongside the river, running wildly through the brush and fallen trees.

The shotgun blast woke Colt fully. He struggled with his horse as it spooked and tried to move away. Regaining control of the animal, he quickly spun it in a small circle and swung into the saddle. Drawing his pistol, Colt spurred Buck forward, racing across the bridge.

Hale was right about the driver being focused on him, but things hadn't gone the way Hale had planned. The driver stared trancelike at Gordy as he lay on the ground unconscious. He believed Hale to be dead and didn't realize that a man was charging at him from behind. The sound of pounding hooves jolted the driver out of his trance, and he turned toward Colt, fully intending to shoot the other barrel of his shotgun at whoever appeared in his sight.

Colt saw the driver turn toward him, and he quickly snapped off a shot at the man. Pitching forward in the wagon, the driver tumbled to the ground. The wagon team moved forward a few yards before stopping, relatively undisturbed by what had just occurred around them. As the driver lay on the ground moaning loudly and clutching at his head, Colt glanced over at Hale. It didn't look good at all.

Galloping up to the driver, Colt brought his horse to a quick stop, the animal wild-eyed and snorting because of the sudden chaos. He burst out of the saddle and landed on the ground with a thud, pointing his pistol at the man.

"Get your hands up! You shot my partner, fella. I'm thinkin' about doing you in right now. I don't know how you're still alive after getting shot in the head like that."

The driver slowly sat up and looked at Colt, his head bleeding profusely, his mind foggy from the hard blow of the bullet grazing him.

"What in the hell is going on here? You can't do something like this!"

"Well, I'm doing it, knucklehead. I'm gonna tie you up and then get at whatever money you have in that mail wagon. Maybe I'll string you up for shootin' my partner. You're dealing with the Cottonwood Kid now. Watch yourself. Say ... I have a question for ya. Are you Norwegian?"

"What?! Norwegian? What in the world does that have to do with anything? My family's from Germany. Do you have something against Norwegians? That's crazy. This entire business is lunacy, and I've never heard of any Cottonwood Kid."

"My pa said a lot of them live in this area. I was just wondering if you were one of them. It's all the same to me. I'm after loot. Now shut up. I'm not liking your attitude much. I need to get over to my partner and get the rope. Stand up."

Colt gestured with his pistol, and the driver struggled to his feet. The two men began walking to where Gordy lay on the ground. The driver staggered along like a drunk in front of Colt, still bleeding profusely. As they approached the seemingly dead bandit, Hale heard them and suddenly sat up.

Gordy looked around, his head moving wildly side to side, fear etched on his face beneath his mask, still not quite convinced he was alive. He couldn't see anything. The mask was askew, the openings for the eyes and mouth out of place.

Satisfied that he was among the living, he

exhaled and said, "Whoa, Nelly! I thought I might be in hell when I first opened my eyes. Couldn't see nothing. But then I smelled that sweet grass and knew I was still here. I'm a little sore. That was one helluva of a tumble. Knocked me straight out. Are you there, Kid? Did you get your job done?"

Colt chuckled as he said, "I sure did, Preacher. Shot this fella right in the head. He sure has a hard head. The bullet ricocheted off it. It's hard to believe."

Hale stood up, brushing himself off as he straightened. He put his mask in order and retrieved his hat, pulling it tightly down into place. Then he walked over to the driver, pulled the man's hand away from his head, and looked at the wound.

"You just grazed him. He'll bleed a little, but be fine. Might have a little scar. You'd think by the way he's moping about that he wasn't long for this earth."

The driver shook his head in disbelief. "I'm getting robbed by a preacher! I've never heard of such a thing. A man of the cloth robbing folks. And my head hurts plenty, thanks to you characters."

Hale snapped at the captive. "Be quiet,

blockhead. Preacher is just my outlaw name. Every outlaw has to have a name. Don't you know that? Let's get over to that wagon and see what we got."

The three men trudged over to the wagon, Colt's spurs tapping out a melody as they walked. The driver led the way, now moving more steadily as he slowly regained his faculties. Crimson fluid had seeped through his clothes and coated his face in a gruesome mask of red, causing him to look like a creature straight out of a nightmare.

They reached the wagon, and Hale hoisted himself into the back. He scanned the contents while Colt kept watch over the driver, pistol held steady in his grip.

Hale looked to Colt and said, "There are bags of mail and a strongbox. We can't take everything, Kid. Do you want to go through some of this mail and see if there's any money in it?"

"No, Preacher. I don't think it'd be right to go through folks' private mail. It seems like an unchristian thing to do."

"You're right, Kid. Let's stick to opening up that strongbox. It looks like there's a pretty good lock on it, but I can probably break it with a couple of shots from my trusty pistol."

Beneath their makeshift masks, both Gordy and Colt were smiling, enjoying their banter using their outlaw names.

Colt had a thought. He squinted his eyes beneath his mask and cocked his pistol. He stood rigidly, staring at the driver. "You got a key for that strongbox? We'll get it open one way or another. Makes no difference to me. I'll shoot your ass if you don't have a key to open it. We're already in this pretty deep. Your life doesn't mean much, but the Preacher, being a religious man, probably doesn't want to see you shot down."

The forceful display frightened the driver. The strongbox wasn't worth dying over. "Yes … Yes. Please don't shoot me! I have a key. It's in my vest pocket. Let me get at it … I won't try nothing. I promise."

The driver reached into his vest pocket and handed Colt the key. Colt tossed the key up to Hale, and he unlocked the box.

If Gordy's face had been visible at that moment, one would have seen unrestrained joy. "We hit the jackpot, Kid! There's paper money and plenty of silver coins. Enough to fund more adventurin', that's for sure. Let's get the driver tied up, and we'll collect our loot and get the hell out of here. The man upstairs sure smiled at us today! Amen."

Hale jumped down from the wagon and bound the driver hand and foot. Sufficiently convinced that the captive could not be of any bother or pose any risk to them, both men climbed into the back of the wagon. They greedily stuffed paper money and coins into their pockets. It wasn't a huge amount, but to Colt and Gordy, it was a fortune. Certainly, it was enough to fund a big night of fun. Completing their task, they jumped to the ground and shook hands. Gordy did a jig and clapped loudly, dancing to a favorite tune playing in his head.

"Damn, Kid! This sure worked out better than I thought it might. We struck the mother lode. Let's gather up that horse of mine and head out. He spooked a little, but I don't think he went too far. He's not much of a runner."

"Sounds good, Preacher. It's not wise to waste any more time. Come to think of it, let's use that leather lariat of mine to bind this fella to one of the wagon wheels. We can't be too careful. I can sure afford to get another one made now."

After binding the driver to a wagon wheel, Colt rode off to retrieve Hale's horse while Hale stayed at the wagon. Colt brought the horse back in short order, Hale mounted up, and the two bandits tipped their hats to the driver before riding off toward Melville.

They rode toward the town at a leisurely pace. There was no hurry, as both men were secure in their belief that the wagon driver would not be discovered for many hours. There was no basis, in fact, for this belief. The driver had been left on the trail from Melville to Big Timber, and this trail was heavily used. Colt thought they would, at some point, leave the trail to Melville and head to Gordy's place to hide out for a while. But Hale had other plans in mind.

"Colt, this money is burning a hole in my pocket. Let's head into Melville and have a little fun before headin' to the home place. What good was doing this job if we can't have some fun? Let's get these stinking masks off. We don't need them anymore."

The two men removed the cloth bags from their heads. Gordy handed Colt his bag, and Colt stuffed them into a saddlebag. He then looked at Hale with concern.

"I don't know, Gordy. Going to Melville doesn't sound like a good idea. We just robbed the mail wagon from that place. At some point, the law is going to be looking for us."

Hale was dismissive. He absolutely believed that everything was going their way. "They don't even know who the hell we are, Colt. That blockhead never saw our faces. Aren't you itching to have a little fun before we have to hole up at the ranch? Besides, I'm plum out of whiskey. I need to pick some up. Life is pretty rough out at the place without a tug on the bottle to soften things up."

"Alright, I'm game. But I want to pick up a new suit of clothes or at least a different hat. Do they have a dry goods store there? I'm the Cottonwood Kid, a known man, and folks are out looking for me. Plus, I want you to be calling me Mr. Howard in town."

Hale looked at his partner, puzzled by what Colt had said. "Yeah, they got a dry goods store there. Mr. Howard? Why do you want me to call you that? Do you have some kinfolk who go by that name?"

"Nope. I just wanna be called that."

"Why? It don't make any sense. Why not just call you Kid?"

"Folks might associate Kid with Cottonwood Kid and be on to us."

"Alright. But why use the name Mr. Howard?"

"I don't wanna tell you."

Hale raised his voice. "For cryin' out loud, Colt. Just tell me. What's the big mystery?"

Colt reluctantly said, "I want to be called Mr. Howard because that's what Jesse James called himself when he went to town."

Hale looked to the sky, as though the answer to Colt's strange behavior would be found there. "You gotta be kidding me! Do you think you're Jesse James now? We better find some cowardly fool in Melville to shoot you down then. If we can't find someone, I'll do it. What do you think of that idea?"

"Thanks, Gordy, but I don't need anybody shooting me down."

"I'll tell you one thing, Colt. I bet ole Jesse never got blown off his horse by a blockhead like that wagon driver."

Both men laughed.

"I reckon that's the truth, Gordy."

Colt looked around. "It sure is pretty in this area. These mountains are something to see. I've always had a special place in my heart for this land. There can't be too many places like it."

Gordy nodded, but said nothing. They continued their ride into Melville in peaceful silence.

MELVILLE

Gordy and Colt pulled their horses to a stop at the end of the main street in Melville. They looked at the bustle of the small town with excitement. Wagons and people crowded the street, hats bobbing like buoys in the bay. The sounds of laughter and music from the saloons were borne on the soft breeze. Gordy looked at Colt, teeth flashing in the sunlight, his eyes glittering. He couldn't believe how lucky he had been on this day, and he meant to take advantage of it.

Colt's father had been correct. Nestled in the shadows of the Crazy Mountains, Norwegians had originally settled Melville, venturing into Montana during territorial days.

Unlike Colt's belief, there was nothing suspicious about their behavior. The settlers had simply been looking for quality ranch land. Melville served as a local center for trading and recreation. It was home to a hotel, four saloons, and various other businesses. Over time, the community had developed a reputation as a rowdy, rough town.

Colt was thinking about his situation more now. Only the adventuring part mattered when he first started on his fresh path in life. There was little thought given to consequences. Now the potential consequences were weighing on him, like a ball and chain around his ankle that grew larger with every passing day. He realized it would be impossible to stay in the area without a terrible end.

Gordy chuckled and said to Colt, "You ready to tear this place up, Mr. Howard? I haven't been to town in a while. Money has been a bit tight."

Colt stared straight ahead, his face devoid of emotion. "Sure. But before we hit the saloons, I think I will get a haircut and a shave. Buy some new clothes and a new hat. Hell, if they have a bath, I will even get one of those before I go into the saloons. I need to change my look a bit. I'll get rid of the chaps and spurs, too. Try to look more like a sheep tender."

Gordy looked sideways at Colt. "Why? Are you looking to be a sheep tender? The ladies aren't too impressed by that. They like cowboys."

Colt shrugged. "I don't know. Thoughts are spinning in my head. I need to give myself a little cover. People will be looking for me now. At least they'll be looking for the cowboy version of the Cottonwood Kid. Changin' my look is like giving me some brush to hide in. People won't be able to see me so easy. As for the women, I got a gal I'm kinda sweet on, so no fancy saloon ladies for me."

"You gotta gal? Who is she?"

"Janel Evinrude. Her dad owns the J-Bar-T over by Shawmut."

This news surprised Gordy. "I know the name. Damn, Colt. Pretty soon you'll be all married up. I didn't know you were the kind of guy to just run to the preacher and get married. I'm more of the walking kind."

A small smile crossed Colt's face, and his mood lightened. "No, Gordy. You're more the kind to go around the preacher. It surprises the hell out of me that you're actually hitched."

Gordy laughed loudly. "That's for sure. The marriage business is a tough trade for me."

Pointing to the activity in the town, Hale said, "Let's get moving and get into town before they find that wagon driver. Then we'll head back to the home place and sit things out."

"Gordy, I'm thinking about heading over to Martinsdale and getting on the train to go west. Get away from the heat that is sure to come down on us. Then, I'll start working back to the east. My gal is heading back to New York City. Maybe that's where I need to be. She's in the moving picture business. She says I have a future in it as a cowboy."

Gordy couldn't believe what he was hearing from Colt, and the loudness of his voice as he spoke reflected that disbelief. "What in the world? You ain't no city man. You're a cowhand. If you go to the city, they'll put those Pinkertons on you. Those gents will hunt you down quickly. You're better off stayin' out here in the open country. I don't know much about moving pictures. I heard a guy talking about it in the Songbird. They say it's quite a sight to see."

"Janel says it's the future. You can do all kinds of things and be all kinds of people in the moving pictures, and they pay you for it. They even had folks rob a train and made a moving picture of it. It was all legal. People came from everywhere to see it. The money might be pretty good. You never know."

Gordy thought for a moment. His face contorted as he considered Colt's plans. "I'm not buying it, Colt. It seems like a foolish thing to do. You're outlawed up now. The law ain't never going to forget that. Maybe a guy can hide in the big city. I don't know how you're going to hide if you join up with the moving pictures."

"I'm Mr. Howard now, Gordy. Remember? I'll be Mr. Howard in New York City too. For all anyone will know, the Cottonwood Kid will still be running around in Montana somewhere."

Gordy threw a hand up. He'd had enough conversation; it was time for action. "It's your deal, Colt. Right now, the only moving I want to do is toward the hotel to get some grub and then to the Songbird. That's my favorite place in town, and they treat me good there. Lord knows I've spent enough money in that place."

He tapped his horse lightly with his feet and said, "Let's go. Time's not on our side. Once they find that driver, the law will come in this direction. I wanna be gone when that happens. Right now, the only information out there is that the Cottonwood Kid and the Preacher pulled that job. We need to keep it that way."

The two men meandered up the main street of town, their horses clip-clopping in perfect cadence. Looming above the other buildings in Melville, McMillan Hotel beckoned to them. Its white wooden facade stood out in stark contrast to its rustic surroundings. When they reached the hotel, they tied the horses to the hitching post and wiped their boots on a mat before entering. The faint aroma of food tickled their noses and pulled them into the hotel like a siren's song.

* * *

GORDY'S STOMACH let out a low growl as they took a seat in the dining room. His mouth watered at the smell of steak and potatoes wafting from nearby plates. Colt remained uninterested at first, lost in thought, until his nose filled with the savory aroma. Then he felt hunger growing in the pit of his stomach. They both ordered steak and potatoes, anxiously shifting in their seats while they waited for the food to arrive. As soon as the server placed the food on the table, Gordy attacked his plate, eating with ravenous hunger. Colt joined in with an equally animalistic fervor, as if it were his last chance for nourishment.

Satiated by the delicious meal, Colt sat back in his chair. "That sure was good. There is nothing like a hot meal when you've been without one for a while. I bet rich folks never understand that."

Gordy nodded. "That's a fact. What's next?"

"Like I said. I'm gonna see about some new clothes and then hit the barber shop for some grooming."

"You sure are going to look different, Colt. I'm heading straight for the Songbird. Meet me over there when you're done getting changed up. I'll have the whiskey ready to go and they always have a good card game. I'm lookin' to build on this pot of gold we just came into."

The men paid for their meal and left the hotel. They paused for a moment outside the building, taking in the bustle, and then Hale waved goodbye to Colt, crossing the street to the Songbird. His step was quick and bouncy, full of excitement, like a child heading to the carnival. Colt grinned at Gordy's display of exuberance and looked around. He saw a sign for the mercantile store and started walking in that direction.

* * *

HEADING toward the barbershop after completing his purchases at the mercantile, Colt looked down at a new shirt, trousers, and derby hat. He suddenly felt light as a feather; he held a new start in his hands. As Colt passed a boy on the street, he took off his cowboy hat and attempted to hand it to the youngster. The boy took a step back, not taking the hat.

Colt spoke gently to the boy. "I won't be

needing this anymore, son. Go ahead and take it."

Seeing that the child was still uneasy, he said, "It's OK, I'm feeling generous today, and you look like a young man who is going to do some cowboying. I know about these kinds of things, and you look like a regular hand to me."

The boy looked at Colt suspiciously, not knowing if he should accept the gift or why it was even being offered. He hesitated for a moment, looking at the ground, pondering the strange situation. But he overcame his doubts, took the hat, and put it on, pulling it down over his ears. Colt could barely see the boy's eyes under the low brim, but the child's toothy grin told the entire story. He thanked Colt for the hat.

Colt laughed at the spectacle. "Dang, son. You look like a genuine cowboy now. Have a good day and take care of that hat. I was always fond of it."

The Cottonwood Kid put on his new derby hat and continued down the street with a smile.

* * *

ENTERING THE BARBER SHOP, Colt immediately noted a lack of customers. *Good. I won't have to wait around for service. The Songbird is singing to me more and more, and it sure is a pretty song.*

The barber was sitting in the barber chair reading a newspaper. The sun streamed in through the window, illuminating motes of dust that danced in the air. A white porcelain basin gleamed brightly, looking as though it had just been purchased and placed in the shop. The entire room smelled of soap, and the floor was dusty, save where footprints led from the door. A broom stood in the corner, its pristine condition speaking to a lack of regular use.

The barber looked up at his new customer with a smile. His nose was red, and it was apparent to Colt that he must have already had a few nips on the bottle.

Putting down his newspaper, the barber pleasantly addressed Colt. "Hello, sir. How can I be of assistance today?"

Colt was equally pleasant in his reply. "Good day to you, too. I'm in the market for a shave, haircut, and a hot bath."

The barber nodded. "I believe we can provide those services. Take a seat, and we'll start with the haircut and shave. I'll have my assistant start on some hot water for a bath. Just a moment."

The barber disappeared into a back room, and Colt heard muffled voices and some laughter. He removed his derby hat and waited in the barber chair, its deep-green leather worn and cracked in places from years of service. He slouched down, his legs dangling off the end. The barber soon returned and began his usual tasks, starting with the haircut. His eyes trailed up and down Colt as he worked, searching for something familiar about the young man in the chair. Nothing triggered any recognition, but he was curious about his customer. The young man had walked in with a new suit of clothes in his hands, and he was dressed oddly. From the neck down, he was all cowboy. The derby hat on his head had seemed out of place.

The barber casually said, "If I may be so bold, young man, what are you doing in the area?"

The question made Colt a little nervous, but he tried to answer disinterestedly. "Oh,

I'm just passing through. I'm headed down to Big Timber to visit some kin and thought I should get gussied up a bit."

"Hmm. What name do you go by? I know a fair number of people in Big Timber. Maybe I know some of your kin."

Colt responded curtly, his nervousness turning to annoyance at the barber's nosy behavior. "I go by the name of Howard. You probably don't know any of my kin. They're the sort of people who keep to themselves."

The barber took the hint that Colt wasn't in the mood for questions. He finished the haircut and shave in silence, then led Colt to the back room where a hot bath awaited him. Colt's eyes sparkled with happiness as he looked at the steam coming off the tub of water.

He took off his dirty clothes and chaps, removed the spurs from his boots. Colt would discard them in short order. He didn't like the thought of getting rid of these items, but it was necessary. This was no time to get waylaid by nostalgia. He kept his bandana. Nobody would think anything of that, and it was useful.

Colt set his new pair of trousers and shirt

on a chair. He hung his derby hat on a hook on the wall, then stepped into the tub, slowly immersing himself in the water. It had been a long time since he had sat in a hot bath, and the experience was quite a luxury. He reveled in it, all the tension in his body melting away. The hot water made him sleepy, and he dozed, thinking of nothing in particular. He didn't know that a local rancher had found the wagon driver as he sat in the tub, relaxing.

* * *

Pushing open the swinging doors to the Songbird, Colt stepped inside. Blinking against the murky light, he searched for Gordy. It was a typical Montana saloon of the times, its patrons beginning to work toward the crescendo of the evening, fueled by a seemingly never-ending supply of alcohol.

A mixture of talking, laughing, and joking echoed off the walls. Young women newly arrived from parts undisclosed moved freely among the men, flirting openly, offering dances and companionship for a price. A card game was just getting started in a small room in the front of the building. Many things had been outlawed in Montana by 1910, but as long as folks kept questionable activities relatively quiet and placed sufficient money in the right hands, people were still free to explore their vices. And the owner of the Songbird was a vigorous advocate of personal freedom.

Colt spotted Gordy Hale waving from the bar. With a wide grin, he walked over and eased up to the bar next to him, leaning on the highly polished wood. Hale slapped Colt on the back.

"Well, how are you doing, Mr. Howard? You look like a sheep-tending fool. It's amazing what a bath, a shave, and a few clothes can do to change a man's look. I thought you'd never show up. I've been holding up this bar for a while now, and it's gettin' heavy."

Colt could see that Hale was already well into a bottle of whiskey, and he snickered. He raised a palm toward Gordy in mock concern. "You need to slow down a bit, partner, or folks will have to carry you out of here. I was hoping I looked like a sheep tender now, and that suits me just fine."

Hale puffed out his chest. "Don't worry about me, Mr. Howard. I can handle my booze better than anybody, and I'm just getting started." He then doubled over, laughing. "You sure look like a man who wants to chase sheep around."

Done laughing, Hale suddenly straightened up, turned around, raised his glass to the saloon patrons, and yelled loudly, "Hard drinkers, drink hard!"

A cheer went up among the crowd. Hale flashed a grin at Colt and waved at the bartender.

"Barkeep. Get my man here a glass. He looks a little thirsty."

The bartender brought Colt a glass, set it down on the bar, and looked at Hale.

"Who's your friend?"

"This is the famous Mr. Howard."

The bartender frowned. "Never heard of him."

"You will, friend. You will."

Hale turned to Colt. "I'm thinking about gettin' in the card game. Do you want to join me?"

"Nah, I'll stay here and jaw with the locals for a while. Have at it."

Hale's eyes lit up. "I tell ya, if I hit it big in that card game, I'm gonna be on easy street. That's for sure."

Colt smirked. "OK, partner. Have some fun. I'll be right here."

Hale did a little dance as he headed to the card room, grabbing a young saloon lady and giving her a big kiss before continuing on his way.

* * *

ONCE INSIDE THE ROOM, Gordy quickly grabbed an open seat. He looked around at his fellow players, mostly known, but there was one unfamiliar face at the table—a man dressed in fine clothes who Hale took to be a professional gambler. The man wore no hat, and his hair was combed back from his forehead and oiled to stay neat, sculpting his features like marble: white skin, blue eyes, thin lips. Hale noted his hands were soft and manicured, having never known much hard work. Gordy immediately disliked him.

Ignoring his newly perceived adversary, Gordy addressed the rest of the group at the table. "Good evening, gents. What's the game?"

The man dealing the cards replied, "The game is five card draw, Gordy. A game we know you're familiar with."

Gordy tapped the table lightly with his palm. "You betcha. That'll work. Deal me in on the next hand."

Hale was an enthusiastic gambler, but not a good card player. He was always welcome at the card table because of his generosity in donating to the pot. Every poker game needs a player who will feed the pot before the serious play begins in a hand, and Gordy filled that role admirably. His typical evening ended with him broke and drunk, with drunkenness usually being attained first. But like any gambler, he had his good days, and those sporadic good days kept him going.

Convinced of his luck on this day, Gordy pulled a wad of paper money out of his pocket, along with some silver dollars, and placed it on the table. Hale wasn't worried about putting a large amount of money on the table; he patted his revolver and smiled. Those seated around the table raised an eyebrow. No one had seen

Hale with this much money in hand. However, a card table is not a place to inquire into an individual's finances, and neither was the Songbird, so the other players kept their mouths shut and continued the game.

Things started well for Hale. He was winning hand after hand. Gordy had another bottle of whiskey brought to the table, imbibing freely. His enthusiasm grew, and his play became more erratic. Losing followed, along with an increasingly sour mood and a dwindling pile of money.

Although Hale didn't know it, his last hand at the Songbird was about to begin. The dealer began passing cards around the table. When he got to Hale, the dealer accidentally flipped the card halfway up before it fell face down in front of Gordy. It was unclear who, if anyone, had seen the card. Still, Hale was outraged.

"Whoa, dealer! That hand needs to be re-dealt. You flipped that card up on the deal."

The other players at the table threw their hands up at Hale's declaration. One man smiled at him and said, "Come on, Gordy. Nobody saw the card. Let's keep playing.

There's no need for the hand to be dealt again."

Hale looked at the man, suspicion in his eyes. "That's because you're holding something good, and now you know what I got. I know you characters don't have a problem cheatin' me if it'll put money in your pocket."

The man in the fine clothes was in fact what Gordy took him to be, a professional gambler. He condescendingly looked at Hale, and the look in the man's eyes made Gordy feel belittled before a word was even spoken. "There's no need to deal the hand again. Nobody here was paying enough attention to know the card. Take it easy. You're getting worked up over nothing, son. Act like a real player."

Gordy's eyes narrowed, and he stared at the man hard. "Don't call me son. Go to hell, Mr. Fancy. I want this no-good hand dealt again."

The gambler threw his head back, and then glared at Gordy, his entire body exuding disgust. "Good grief, you sure are an insolent fella."

The man had gone a step too far. Hale quickly stood up, drew his pistol, and shot the gambler in the chest. There was a momentary pause before a large, muscular card player next to Hale tackled him, pinning Gordy's arms to his side.

The large man yelled, "Somebody help me! Don't just sit there!"

Chaos ensued as two other men joined in the fray, the group rolling around on the floor as they tried to bring Gordy under control. Hale was strong, but the three men finally subdued him and got his weapon away. As Gordy was being held down, another man ran out to his horse and retrieved some piggin' strings. Soon Gordy's hands were tied behind his back, but this didn't relieve his fury. He struggled mightily against his restraints.

"Let me go! You ain't the law! These strings are too tight. Loosen them up a bit."

The large man replied, "Sorry, Gordy. You just shot a man. You ain't going anywhere until we fetch the law. Now, settle down. There's no use in struggling. You're not getting away from us."

Looking at Gordy's victim lying on the floor, the large man said, "How's that fella doing?"

Upon being shot, the gambler had fallen forward into the table, knocking it over and ending up on his side. One of the card players quickly rolled him on his back, examined him, and gave his prognosis. "He's dead!"

The large man looked around at the group in the card room. "Somebody go fetch the deputy right now."

A voice came from the middle of the room. "I'll go get him." The individual said no more, pushed his way to the front, and rushed out of the room in search of the deputy.

A small crowd formed outside the card room as everyone waited anxiously for the law to appear. At this point in the proceedings, Colt was on the far end of the saloon, engrossed in a conversation with a fellow patron, when a young woman rushed up to them.

Without introducing herself, she breathlessly reported, "A man named Gordy Hale shot a feller in the card room. He's dead as can be! The law will be here soon. Anyone on the scout better get gone now!" Her declaration finished, she hurried off to warn others.

Colt tried to remain as calm as possible.

The saloon had been so loud that the pop of the gun didn't really register with him. It didn't take long for the gravity of the situation to become clear. This was bad news, terrible news.

He shook the hand of the man he was talking to, excused himself, and quietly slipped out the front of the saloon. He glanced toward the card room as he left, but couldn't see anything because of the crowd. Nobody paid any attention to him; everyone was focused on the drama unfolding in the card room.

Several minutes passed before the deputy arrived at the saloon, and then Gordy Hale was removed by a group of men, kicking and yelling as he was roughly coerced toward the small jail in Melville. As he was being pushed and dragged toward the jail, Gordy looked out into the street and saw a man in a derby hat ride by on his Appaloosa, nodding at him as he passed. He started laughing maniacally and fought his captors even harder.

* * *

ONCE OUTSIDE THE SONGBIRD, Colt scurried back to the hotel, where the horses were still tied. His eyes darted from building to building, as if he were expecting someone to jump out from a hidden spot and place him under arrest at any moment. Gordy's fate seemed sealed, but Colt felt he still had a chance to escape.

Reaching the horses, he removed his derby hat for a moment and ran his hand through his hair, exhaling slowly to calm himself. Nobody in Melville knew him, and now he had altered his appearance enough not to be recognized as the Cottonwood Kid. However, there was a large question looming. Would Gordy keep his mouth shut and give him enough time to outrun the law?

Quickly unhitching his horse, he put a foot in the stirrup and was just about to swing into the saddle when he paused. He put his foot back on the ground and patted Buck on the neck. He had to switch horses. Colt looked over at Gordy's Appaloosa, still standing quietly at the hitching post. It would have to do.

Stealing a horse now might raise more alarm, and the Cottonwood Kid was last seen on a buckskin. Colt reasoned people wouldn't be looking for him on a different horse. Sadness suddenly filled him as he realized this would be the last time he would see his trusty steed.

"I think this is where we say goodbye, old friend. Things are getting too hot for me. Folks will know by now that I'm riding a buckskin. I need to switch mounts. Gordy won't be needing this Appaloosa anymore."

He glanced around quickly, looking for anything out of place. "I need to make the train in Martinsdale, and I can clear the territory. My adventurin' around here is done. I'm heading out to work my way to Janel in the east. I'll head west on the train, look around a bit, and then circle back to the east. Nobody will know me in New York. I'll try to break into the moving picture business when I get there. You were always the best, Buck. Don't worry, there will never be another one like you. I wish you luck."

Colt untied the Appaloosa and led both horses to a spot out of sight of the main street. Gordy's saddle wouldn't work for him, so he unsaddled both horses and put his saddle on the Appaloosa. Colt left Gordy's saddle and other gear lying on the ground. He tied Buck to a post. Colt thought the horse might follow him, and he didn't need an extra horse tagging along, especially a buckskin. He assumed that with all the commotion surrounding Gordy, no one would pay attention to a lone rider leaving town, and if Gordy could keep his mouth shut for a bit, he might make it out of Melville.

He rode the Appaloosa slowly up the main street, appearing unhurried. Just another person leaving town for a ranch in the surrounding area. As Colt rode up the street, he saw Gordy being hauled out of the Songbird, heading in the opposite direction. Everybody in the street watched Hale fighting and cursing the men who were moving him toward the jail. When Colt was even with Hale, Gordy looked straight at him. Colt nodded and continued his way out of Melville. The town was none the wiser that they had played host to the Cottonwood Kid.

* * *

HALE WAS HUSTLED into the small, dimly lit office area of the jail. A sour scent of sweat and mildew filled his nostrils as two men, their hands like iron grips around his biceps, held him. The lone cell door creaked and groaned as it was unlocked and opened with a shrill, metallic screech. Once that task was completed, the bindings were removed from Gordy's hands, causing welts to rise on his skin like mountain ridges, and the men threw him into the cell without ceremony, the door rattling behind him.

The deputy pulled a chair up to the cell, sitting in silence, his gaze unwavering and cold as ice. Hale sat down on a worn bed that creaked under his weight, its wooden frame battered and splintered. The deputy continued to stare at Hale, trying to measure him and formulate a plan for his interrogation. He knew Hale from previous dealings for minor infractions, and the deputy thought he had a pretty good handle on Gordy's character. After an uncomfortable silence, steeped in apprehension for Gordy, the questioning began.

"It looks like you're in a tough spot, Hale. In the old days, you'd be strung up for sure. But now that we're living in the new days of law and order, you might escape the noose. Then again, maybe not."

Hale's apprehension turned to defiance. "You're full of it, lawman. What the hell are you even talking about? I shot a man in an illegal card game who was going to shoot me. It's plain old self-defense. I didn't have no choice. I'll take that in front of a judge any day."

The deputy spat on the floor. "It's not just the shooting that's the problem. I've been told you were sportin' a lot of cash in that card game. You aren't a man known to have a big stake."

Gordy shrugged. "So what? I had some money. Is it illegal for a man to have money now? What kind of world are we livin' in these days? Nobody seemed to mind when I was divvying it up on the table."

The deputy rubbed his chin, then paused for dramatic effect. "It's curious that you suddenly have a big stake for a poker game right after someone robbed the mail wagon earlier today."

Hale's body stiffened, and he nervously looked away from his interrogator. "I don't know anything about a mail wagon robbery. Don't try to pin that crap on me."

The deputy chuckled. "Well, the mail wagon driver says you know something about it. He was found earlier today, and I spoke with him after the doctor fixed the bullet crease on his head. The driver says you and some character calling himself the Cottonwood Kid robbed the mail wagon."

Hale laughed derisively at this suggestion, regaining his defiant attitude. "That's a lie. I ain't no robber. You can ask anyone around."

The deputy continued calmly. "The driver says the Kid used your name during the holdup."

"What? The Kid never used my name during it."

There was a long pause. The deputy smiled at Hale, and Hale realized, even in his drunken state, that he had messed up badly. His bravado turned to despair, and he wept, putting his face in his hands.

After a few moments, Hale composed himself and said, "I've stepped in it big this time. I'm done for. I have a wife and kids who depend on me, and now they'll be out in the cold while I rot behind bars."

The deputy remained silent, looking at Hale. Gordy stared at the filthy, scuffed floor and sighed.

Maintaining his silence for a while longer, making sure that Hale fully felt his predicament, the deputy said, "I might be able to help you out, Gordy, but you gotta come clean with me. Tell me everything I want to know. Understand? No messing around."

Hale looked up. "Alright, alright. I did it. I did the mail wagon robbery with the Cottonwood Kid. Can you help me out? I got a family."

"You must have been the man calling himself the Preacher, is that right?"

Hale nodded. "That's right. But I don't remember the Kid calling me by my real name during the robbery. I told the Kid not to use my real name and I'm sure he didn't. We had masks on the whole time. The wagon driver didn't see our faces."

"Focus now, Gordy. OK? The driver said the Cottonwood Kid is a tall, duded-up cowboy who rides a buckskin horse. Is that correct?"

Hale didn't answer right away. He closed his eyes and mumbled to himself, rocking slowly, the squeaking of the bed marking the tempo. His hands were clenched tightly together, as though he were praying.

Then Gordy relaxed, looked the deputy straight in the eye and said, "He's a cowboy, alright. He believes in the old ways of cowboying. If you want to call that duded-up, then yeah, he's a duded-up cowboy. He rides a nice buckskin horse, too. That's right."

"How did you come to know him?"

His emotions now under control, Gordy spoke evenly. "He was riding the grub line, I guess. Showed up at my place looking for somewhere to sleep and something to eat. Delilah cooked him up a mess of food, and we got into the bottle a little. He told me about a job he wanted to do over by Melville. That there was a mail wagon that would be easy to knock off. I knew the area, so I threw in with him."

"What's his real name?"

"He never said, and I didn't ask. It's not polite to ask something like that. He would've volunteered it if he wanted me to know his name."

The deputy persisted in his questioning. "Did he come into Melville with you?"

"Nope. After the job, we parted ways, and he lit out for the hills. He said he was headed for the Castle Mountains. He was going to lie low there for a while."

"So, we're looking for a duded-up cowboy on a buckskin horse?"

Hale nodded in agreement. "Yep. Duded-up as hell. A real fancy-looking cowboy."

"Young or old?"

"I'd say he might be tending toward the older side, but I didn't ask him his age."

The deputy stood up and looked at one of the men. "I need to get a message to Sheriff Bates down in Big Timber and Sheriff Sedgwick up in Meagher County. I think he stays mostly in Harlowton, but we'll also send a message to White Sulphur Springs to be sure he gets it. You stay here and keep an eye on this place while I'm gone. Alright, I'm heading out."

The deputy quickly left the jail and headed off on his errand. Gordy stretched out on the bed and stared up at the ceiling. He smiled a little and closed his eyes.

* * *

LATER THAT NIGHT, a message arrived in Harlowton. However, it failed to be delivered until early the following morning. It read:

To: Sheriff Sedgwick, Meagher County

Mail wagon robbed outside Melville. Be on the lookout for a tall, "duded-up" cowboy on a buckskin horse. Suspect calls himself the Cottonwood Kid. He is thought to be heading for the Castle Mountains. Please assist in the apprehension of this individual. Thank you for your help in this matter. Sincerely, Deputy Hill, Sweet Grass County.

MARTINSDALE

*E*arly in the morning, there was a knock at the door to Sedgwick's office in Harlowton. It was common knowledge that he often slept there on a bed in the corner, so a messenger had dutifully arrived to deliver a telegram.

The loud knock on the door startled Sedgwick, and he sat up quickly, looking around in sleepy confusion. Another knock came with the same urgency, and he rose from his bed, pulling on a pair of trousers and raising the attached suspenders over his shoulders. He walked to the door, unlocked it, and opened it, looking disgustedly at the man standing before him.

"What are you doing here so early? I was having a good sleep before you rousted me out of bed. Did somebody die or something?"

The messenger was unaffected by Sedgwick's demeanor and said, "Good morning, Sheriff Sedgwick. This is a message for you from the deputy down in Melville. It should've been brought to you last night. It seems urgent, so I wanted to get it to you right away. My apologies for it not being brought to you sooner."

The man handed Sedgwick the message, and the sheriff studied it closely. It didn't take long for him to grimace, close his eyes, and groan. He crumpled up the piece of paper and tossed it on the floor.

"Now I'm going to have to hunt this fool cowboy. I need to get over to McCloskey at the Graves and round him up. Are there any trains heading to Martinsdale this morning?"

"Yes, I believe one will be here within the hour."

Sedgwick nodded in approval. "Good. That will save us some hard riding. We'll take the train to Martinsdale and go from there. Thanks for delivering the message. I need to get moving on this situation."

The men shook hands, and the messenger took his leave. Sedgwick hurriedly dressed and gathered the gear necessary for a manhunt. He locked the office and headed down to the Graves.

Arriving at the Graves, he was pleasantly surprised to find McCloskey already up, reading some correspondence over a morning cup of coffee in the dining area. Sedgwick walked up to McCloskey, dumping his gear in a heap in front of the railroad detective.

McCloskey looked up from his papers. "Good morning, Sedgwick. What brings you here so early? I'm a notoriously early riser myself. I wanted to get a start on some correspondence."

"Are you ready for a chase, McCloskey? That crazy cowboy who hit the train robbed the mail wagon outside of Melville. I just got a message that he might be heading into the Castle Mountains. He might pass through Martinsdale on his way. The fool could stop there a spell. But Martinsdale is a good place to base out of if he heads into the Castles from Melville. That's my jurisdiction, so I need to get a handle on this situation. Grab your gear. There's a train leaving for Martinsdale shortly, and we need to be on it."

"Do you think there's a real chance he might stop in Martinsdale before heading into the mountains, or is that just a hope?"

"Who knows, he might have already passed through there. The message arrived a little late. I'm not sure what he's up to now, but he's passed over into being a real outlaw. Don't know if that was his plan, but we need to put a stop to it."

The sheriff paused, the gears in his mind whirling quickly. Satisfied that he had a plan, he said, "I'll get a message to my deputies in White Sulphur Springs and have them meet us in Martinsdale. I can do that at the depot. We'll get mounts and form up a posse for a hunt from there. If we're real lucky, he'll show up in Martinsdale and linger a bit, but I doubt it. There's one thing I know for sure. If we hang around here any longer, we'll miss the train."

McCloskey agreed with that assessment and said, "I'll run to my room and gather my gear. Be right back."

Quickly gathering his correspondence, McCloskey practically bounded up the stairs leading to his room. This surprised Sedgwick and he looked around, wondering if anyone else had witnessed McCloskey's sudden speed. Nothing in the railroad detective's appearance or manner had prepared the sheriff for that display of sudden athleticism.

Waiting impatiently for McCloskey to return, Sedgwick paced back and forth. He looked at McCloskey's half-full cup of coffee, grabbed it, and guzzled it down. Sedgwick was a man who needed a little coffee in the morning to lubricate his mind. He giggled like a child when he finished. Positive it would horrify McCloskey if the detective knew the sheriff had unceremoniously emptied his coffee cup.

It didn't take long for McCloskey to gather his gear, and the two men were on their way to the train depot. The train arrived on time, and after Sedgwick explained the situation to the conductor, the train departed in haste.

* * *

STEPPING off the train in Martinsdale, Sedgwick took in the view. It looked the same as it always did—a sleepy little town smack dab at the epicenter of sheep country in the Upper Musselshell. A person could see all the way up the main street from the train depot. Charlie Bair's place wasn't too far away. In 1910, he would ship forty-seven train cars full of wool to Boston from Montana.

Sedgwick stretched his arms above his head and then looked at McCloskey. "It doesn't look like my deputies have arrived. I guess I didn't really think they would be here yet. We'll have the folks at the depot look after our gear. Let's head up the street to the hotel and get a bite to eat and some coffee. Lord knows I need some. It's a good vantage point. We can see everything from there."

They walked up the street slowly, taking in the beautiful view of the Crazy and Castle Mountains. The sun was rising higher in the sky, illuminating the imposing mountains that acted as a gateway between the sea of blue above and the rich grazing land surrounding the town.

Sedgwick suddenly stopped and waved his arm in a half-circle. "This little town and the surrounding country may not seem like much, but this might be the sheep capital of the entire nation. There's money here. A lot of money. You just don't see it flaunted like you would in the big city. That little bank across the street from the hotel is stuffed full of money. A pretty tempting target, if you ask me."

The sheriff continued walking, and Mc-Closkey followed without comment. They entered the hotel and sauntered into the dining room, which was in the front of the building and had large windows, so that patrons could look out at the town and mountains while they enjoyed their meal. A server seated them at a table with the best view of the main street and the bank. Menus were produced, and both men ordered a hearty breakfast with plenty of coffee to wash it down. When the food arrived, they ate silently for some time, savoring a good meal in a peaceful place.

Sedgwick broke the silence first. "Mc-Closkey, we're both older now. Do you ever think about the old days? Before all this so-called civilized living came along? The politicians always talk about the future and progress, but I liked this country when it was wild and free."

McCloskey took a drink of coffee before replying. "I do think about it, Sedgwick. At least when it comes to the type of criminals we chase. I worked on the robbery of the Great Northern up in Malta by the Wild Bunch. Kid Curry led them in that one; Butch and Sundance were gone by then. I guess I have a certain amount of regard for the real outlaws. They were tough and resourceful men. Not like this Cottonwood Kid character we're after. He seems like little more than a fool."

The sheriff nodded slightly. "I agree with you. I know there are still men out in these hills who rode with outlaws in the old days. But as long as they don't cause trouble any-more, I'm willing to let things lie. Hell, the old days weren't that long ago. This Cottonwood Kid has crossed over the line now. He may be a fool, but even a fool can be dangerous under the right circumstances, and we haven't caught him yet. Maybe we're the fools."

McCloskey laughed. "Maybe so. They say Butch and Sundance are probably dead, but to tell you the truth, I kinda hope they're still out there somewhere."

"Me too, McCloskey, me too."

* * *

IT's a peculiar fact of life that when one strongly believes things to be a certain way, the very thing one seeks will pass right in front of them, unnoticed. And so it was that a tall young man in a derby hat riding an Appaloosa, looking very unlike a "duded-up" cowboy, rode up to the State Bank of Martinsdale, tethered his horse, and calmly walked inside the bank. He drew no attention from the lawmen, who gave him nothing more than a passing glance.

Then, shortly thereafter, an older man came up the street from the opposite direction and entered the bank. It wasn't long before shots could be heard coming from the building. The two lawmen looked at each other, frozen with shock, the seconds ticking by, marking their inaction. Then, recovering their senses, Sedgwick and McCloskey rushed from the hotel to the bank, drawing their pistols as they went.

* * *

COLT WAS in no rush that morning. He had laid up in a coulee outside of Martinsdale that offered some cover and had a good sleep. There were no provisions, but that was no problem. He would soon be on the train, having a sumptuous meal, so a bit of hunger was no bother. No stress was evident in his manner as he rode along, just fatigue from the previous day's activities and a hard ride to Martinsdale. He had no expectation of encountering any law officers, now firm in the belief that Hale wouldn't sell him out. Besides, he looked different now and was on a different horse, not a cowboy on a buckskin.

The notion of robbing the State Bank of Martinsdale came about suddenly. Colt didn't plan to rob anything before arriving on that town's tranquil main street. But then he saw the bank, and his gaze instantly locked on to the building. It was beckoning to him, a golden goose in the form of a small wooden building. How hard could it be? There was little activity on the street and the town was tiny. He quickly calculated that a heist would be incredibly simple, and a getaway easy. Who was going to chase him? There was nobody around. Just when he thought his adventuring days were over, fate had smiled at him and presented an irresistible opportunity. What could go wrong?

Colt smiled as he worked out the possibilities in his mind. After the job, he could head into the Crazy Mountains or the Castles, then work back to another train depot farther west. Switch horses and clothes again; that wouldn't be hard to do. Maybe adopt the look of a traveling businessman. The money would be a good grubstake to get him back to the east, to Janel. He still had a little money from the mail wagon, but it wouldn't last long. If he knocked off this little bank, there would be plenty of money to carry out his plans.

There was no more thinking to be done. Colt calmly rode to the front of the bank, casually dismounted, and tied the Appaloosa to a hitching post. He slid his bandana over his face just after entering the bank and drew his pistol.

* * *

THERE WAS no one in the bank except for the bank clerk, who was standing at the cage, busily writing in a ledger. Colt moved briskly to the cage. When the clerk looked up to acknowledge his customer, a pistol was pointed directly at his face. He froze, eyes dilated with surprise and fear.

There was no tension in Colt's manner. He was becoming comfortable with his new vocation. "Here's the deal, mister. You're going to fill a couple of your money bags up with loot. Be quick about it, and you'll live. Dally, and I'm gonna put a bullet in you."

The clerk didn't immediately move; the sudden, unexpected situation still paralyzed him.

Colt leaned in toward the clerk and said, "Get your ass moving or die. Your choice. I can fill the bags myself if I have to. I'll come right through that damn cage!"

The clerk jolted out of his paralysis and began to work on his task. Colt followed his movements with quiet satisfaction. This was going to be easier than he thought. Just a few quick minutes, and he would be on his way. Then, the door to the bank opened, and in walked another man holding a pistol at the ready, Manuel Vaca.

Colt swung around and faced the new entrant in the heist. Both men pointed their pistols at each other, but neither man fired immediately. The appearance of the Professor stunned Colt. Why was the Professor also trying to rob the bank, and why had he not bothered to cover his face?

Manuel Vaca did not recognize his adversary. The bank clerk stopped what he was doing and looked on in amazement. Two bank robbers? Were they working together?

Colt made the first entreaty. "Put that pistol down. Right now! Just leave, and no harm will come to you. There's nothing here for you."

Vaca was perplexed; not only was someone else trying to rob the bank, but he recognized the voice. "Colt, is that you?"

"No … No, sir. I'm the Cottonwood Kid, and you are messin' up my bank job. Get the hell out of here or suffer the consequences."

"I know it's you, Colt. Put your pistol down. Let's work out a deal. We can both benefit."

"Dang it, Professor! You messed everything up! This is my job, and I ain't sharing."

"Have you lost your mind, Colt? There's plenty of money for both of us. Let's work together, and then we'll head our separate ways. Don't be greedy, amigo."

Colt shook his head vigorously. He wasn't going to share anything. "Nope. Can't do that. I need every bit of this loot for my new start. I'm a wanted man now. Last chance. Lower that pistol and leave."

Vaca couldn't believe Colt's behavior. Why wouldn't he work with him? They both could prosper from the bank robbery. But Vaca's instincts were sharp from his many experiences on the outlaw trail. He wasn't about to be shot down by a half-baked cowboy. He studied Colt's gun hand intensely, looking for the slightest movement that would indicate Colt was going to fire at him.

It didn't take long for the tell to come. Vaca saw Colt's finger twitch on the trigger. He bolted to his right and fired, just as Colt pulled the trigger. A bullet whizzed past Vaca's shoulder, missing him narrowly as it struck the wall behind. Colt slumped down against the bank counter, dropping his gun onto the floor with a thud, his bandana falling off his face. Vaca knew Colt was mortally wounded before he ever hit the floor; his shot had been true. In the silence that immediately followed, a deep sense of melancholy filled Manuel.

"Stupid cowboy. It didn't have to be this way."

Vaca's eyes were locked on Colt when the bank clerk, sensing an opportunity, acted. He slid his hands under the bank counter and fumbled for the sawed-off shotgun hidden there. In his hurry, he accidentally bumped the gun on the counter as he was about to raise it, throwing the barrel off course and clattering metal against wood. It only cost him a second of time, but that time would prove fatal. Vaca heard it and reacted immediately. Like a bolt of lightning, he fired a single shot that struck the clerk in the forehead. The clerk disappeared behind the counter in an instant. Vaca took a slow breath, thankful for his lucky escape. Hopefully, that luck would hold.

The entire affair had taken very little time. Vaca reasoned that he still had enough time to grab some money. He knew he wouldn't have long, though. The gunshots would have alerted the community that something was wrong in the bank. He may even need to shoot his way out of Martinsdale now.

Vaca looked down again at Colt, who was still breathing. He knew Colt was close to the end. The cowboy's chest was moving in time to his shallow, quick breaths. Colt's impending death strangely affected Manuel, who had seen many men die. He reproached himself. What good was it? He had to get going, but he couldn't.

Manuel moved close to Colt and squatted down. He took Colt's hand and held it gently.

Colt looked over at Manuel with glassy eyes that were becoming ever more vacant. "Professor … Did that Spanish fella … Don … I don't remember … Did he go out like this?"

Manuel spoke slowly, each word tinged with sadness. "No, amigo, his journey was different. Everyone's journey is their own. None is the same. We are just boats bobbing in the sea, and we come to shore where the Creator wants. Now, rest. Just rest."

Colt said his last words just above a whisper. "I was heading out to be with my gal in the moving pictures."

Manuel felt Colt's hand go limp. There was no more breath, and the Cottonwood Kid died against a bank counter in a small building in the Upper Musselshell.

* * *

MANUEL STOOD UP. There was still the matter of the money. He needed to get some quick and be on his way. Unfortunately, the sand in the hourglass ran out.

Sedgwick and McCloskey rushed into the bank and immediately aimed their pistols at Manuel.

McCloskey yelled, "Drop the pistol! Hands in the air!"

Vaca did not drop his pistol. He rested his thumb on the hammer and his finger on the trigger, but did not raise the gun. He studied the men, trying to decipher their intentions. A solution to his predicament came to him suddenly, although it pained him.

"I'm not the bandit. The bandit lies dead on the floor. I'm a customer of this bank and was simply here to do business."

McCloskey frowned. "That doesn't cut it with me."

Sedgwick knew Vaca and his history. The sheriff was pretty sure of the situation before him. Manuel would not stand down and be arrested. There was no point in more senseless bloodshed. The money was still in the bank and would remain there. Sedgwick gave Vaca a knowing smile, then holstered his weapon and turned to McCloskey.

"McCloskey, holster your weapon. I know this man. He works the sheep ranches around here. He's been around since the old days and has lived cleanly for some time, as far as I know."

McCloskey glanced at Sedgwick and gave him a confused look before cautiously putting his pistol away.

Sedgwick looked back at Vaca and said, "Professor, it's funny to see you here today. It looks like you just foiled a bank robbery and ended a desperado all in one go. That's the gist of it, isn't it?"

Manuel holstered his pistol slowly and narrowed his eyes, staring at Sedgwick intently. "Yes … Yes, that's the truth of it. I have money in this bank."

"You know, Professor, George Parrott used to ride in this country in olden times before he met his maker down in Wyoming. I think he even had a Mexican riding with him. Went by the name of Manuel Garcia if I remember correctly. Some folks say that man is still around these parts. You wouldn't know anything about that, would you?" Sedgwick stared back at Manuel, then relaxed and shrugged. "Oh hell, those days are long gone now."

Manuel smiled ever so slightly. "I've heard that too, Sheriff Sedgwick. But who knows what could've happened to the man now? He was no relation of mine. You're right, though. Parrott rode here many years ago. I'm surprised anyone knows of him now."

Sedgwick snorted, stopping just short of a laugh. "Yep, it sure was a spell ago. I guess we'll never know what happened to Garcia, will we? All from a bygone time. Do you know this bandit you shot?"

"I don't know the man. He called himself the Cottonwood Kid."

"Where's the bank clerk?"

"The bandit shot him in a fit of rage when the clerk wouldn't cooperate. That gave me the time to draw my pistol and shoot the bandit. The bandit was foolish. He didn't even try to disarm me. I guess the clerk's actions distracted him. The clerk is dead behind the counter."

Sedgwick smiled at McCloskey. "There you go, McCloskey. Case solved."

McCloskey didn't believe any of it, but he knew there was nothing he could do about the situation. He couldn't disprove Vaca's story and the Cottonwood Kid had been way-laid. The railroad wouldn't care about anything other than that fact.

Sedgwick looked at Vaca and said, "I guess we owe you a debt of gratitude. There's reward money available if you want to come into Harlowton and collect it."

"I don't want your blood money. I'll take my leave if that's OK."

"Sure. Suit yourself. Are you sticking around the area?"

"No. I'm heading out of this country. Going south to see my people in the borderlands."

"That sounds like a good idea. Get a fresh start and live among your relations. I wish you luck."

Sedgwick shook Vaca's hand, and Manuel walked out of the bank. The sheriff looked around, and a glum, tired look appeared on his face.

"We've got a mess to clean up here, McCloskey. We better get to it and just get it done. There's nothing ever pleasant about these situations. I suspect you have some paperwork to complete for the railroad afterward. You got your man, and the Milwaukee should be happy about that."

McCloskey responded indifferently, studying a tiny trickle of blood that was trying to work its way into a crack in the floorboards. "Yes, Sedgwick. They'll be happy, and you're right. There's always paperwork to do in the railroad detective business. I'll have to get to it right away. I want to put this matter to rest as soon as possible. Not that it matters, I guess. The work never seems to end."

* * *

MANUEL VACA YANKED his horse away from the hitching post, mounting the saddle in a single leap. He chuckled at this unexpected display of his former youth. Digging his spurs into the animal, the horse galloped away, its hooves pounding against the dry dirt of Martinsdale.

Rushing along, thoughts whirled in his head like a storm, and the wind whispered memories in his ears. His mind traveled back to days when all seemed possible, and freedom surged through Vaca's veins. He rode up the South Fork past Lennep, then a little farther, into the winding pathways of the Shields Valley toward Livingston, and into memory.

EPILOGUE

$\mathcal{M}$any years later, in a mansion in Beverly Hills, an old woman sits in a worn leather chair. Bathed in the light of a silent film, she holds a glass of scotch in her hand. She smiles and gazes, transfixed, at a picture on the wall of Mary Pickford and a young woman, all youth and confidence staring back at her. Next to it is an old movie poster that hung at the American Theatre in Harlowton. *Sagebrush Knight*, starring William S. Hart as the lead.

Memories flood into her mind, memories that become a little fainter with each passing day. Sepia-tinted fragments drift by, and she fears they will float away like wisps of smoke, never to return. A tear streams down her cheek as she thinks of a cowboy who went adventuring so long ago. She wipes the tear away quickly, but then another comes, and another, and she lets them flow freely. Just like she has done on many other days. And she focuses on the young woman on the silver screen in front of her, taking comfort in a beauty that will remain frozen in time forever.

ACKNOWLEDGMENTS

Thanks to everyone who contributed to the production of this book. Especially beta reader Kim Walters, editor Emma Moylan, and the Book Cover Zone.

ABOUT THE AUTHOR

Born in El Paso, TX, and raised in Eastern
Montana, Everett Riggs is a lifelong fan of the
Western genre and the Old West. He attended
college at Montana State University and the
University of Iowa, graduating with degrees
in mathematics and law. He also served with
the U.S. Army in the Persian Gulf War. In his
spare time, he likes to read, write, and enjoy
various outdoor activities with his family.